Cytokine

Uriel and Carolyn Limjoco

Fulton Books, Inc.
Meadville, PA

Published by Fulton Books 2021

This story is fictional. Any resemblance to present or past events is purely accidental. Likewise, all the characters are fictional, and any resemblance to names of people living or deceased is likewise fictional.

ISBN 978-1-64952-528-4 (paperback)
ISBN 978-1-64952-529-1 (digital)

Printed in the United States of America

CHAPTER 1

Los Angeles, California

SEVERAL WOMEN GIGGLE AND GIVE one another Hollywood air kisses. One of the women turns around and gives another woman behind her a Hollywood air kiss. They ignore the unusually stiff Santa Ana winds in February that rustle the red-and-white oleander shrubs and a copse of purple jacaranda trees nearby.

The women are part of a throng of spectators behind security barriers, gawking at the formally attired gods and magnificent, scantily dressed goddesses of Hollywood, arriving for the annual Academy Awards. Limousines drop them off.

Some of them turn around and acknowledge their screaming fans with flying kisses, then disappear inside the Kodak Theatre.

The multitude of fans outside are all eagerly anticipating the arrival of a popular, handsome, and lean sixty-some-year-old actor Forrest Trask.

Trask has the leading male role in the current blockbuster movie *Space Station Zulu*. He is the crowd's choice to receive the Oscar for Best Male Lead Actor.

Trask finally arrives. Accompanied by his lovely wife, he steps out of the limousine, smiling, turns around, and takes some time acknowledging the accolade that is being showered on him by the crowd.

Then he and his wife walk slowly in through the decorated portals of the theater. Only the fortunate few and members of the Hollywood elite are inside the theater to witness and enjoy the ceremony.

The rest of the world can only see the proceedings through live television.

Inside the theater the guests are treated with a lavish, but elegant decor in lavenders and pinks. They are the favorite colors of actress Yolanda Swift, who recently passed away after a very successful seventy-five-year-long movie career. The lights dim, and the ceremony gets started.

For those who are anticipating the awarding of the Oscar for Best Actors, the event seems unceasingly long. But the great moment does come.

On the stage are Clifton Sands, a handsome, but rugged-looking young man, who is quickly identified by the guests for his role in many Western movies, and Roberta Haggerty, a very attractive young lady, who is relatively new in Hollywood. Sands steps closer to the microphone and, with a fully authoritative and clear voice, begins.

"For Best Actor in a Leading Role, the candidates are James Oberstein for *Petitions from the Heart.*"

A short segment of Oberstein in action is shown on two separate, giant screens.

"Robert Greenlee for *Canadian Adventure.*" A short segment of Greenlee in action is shown.

"Forest Trask for *Space Station Zulu.*" A short segment of Trask in action is shown.

"And Darrell Lindsey for *An Affair with Destiny.*" A short segment of Lindsey in action is shown.

"And the Oscar goes to…"

Actress Haggerty receives the envelope and steps up to the microphone, opens it, and reads the name, "Forrest Trask for *Space Station Zulu!*" The audience rises and cheers.

Trask, sixty-eight years old, trim and handsome, energetically gets up onstage and receives his Oscar from Haggerty, who gives him a hug and a kiss on his cheek. Sands congratulates him with a warm and firm handshake. Trask walks up to the microphone and acknowledges his adoring fans with a smile and polite bow.

"For two decades I echoed Bob Hope's lament about this evening as Passover night for me. I finally made it! I want to thank my wife, who gave me the encouragement and confidence I needed, the Academy for this great honor, and the lovely Semantha Stevens, my leading lady, for her outstanding performance." Spotlights pick out Stevens from the audience as she rises and politely acknowledges.

Trask continues, "I also want to thank Dr. Davidson of the Davidson Cancer Research Foundation. Unfortunately, Dr. Davidson cannot be with us tonight because of his busy medical schedule. Only a year ago, I was dying of terminal cancer. Dr. Davidson gave me his sixteen-week regimen of treatments and cleansed me of every cancer cell.

I believe in miracles, especially scientific miracles. Now I feel stronger than I've ever felt in my life! Even my beautiful wife, Crystal, believes that I have been reenergized a hundredfold!"

Spotlights focus on the most attractive and statuesque thirty-four-year-old, blonde Crystal, who rises and politely acknowledges her recognition.

Trask continues, "I am alive today, healthy and energetic. Thank you, Dr. Davidson, who is probably watching me on television, and thanks to all of you."

Trask walks briskly down from the stage, waving his statuette amid cheers and whistles from the audience. He joins with Crystal, and together they examine the trophy as if it were alive.

Crystal whispers to her husband, "Oh, how I wish Dr. Davidson had been here. He would have been very proud of you."

Trask whispers back, "He's so damned dedicated to his work that not even Mr. Oscar himself can pull him out of that building. I only hope he's watching us on TV." Trask and Crystal just smiled.

CHAPTER 2

Davidson Cancer Research Foundation Charleston, South Carolina

THE DAVIDSON CANCER RESEARCH FOUNDATION is housed in an impressive five-story building near Downtown Charleston, South Carolina.

A relatively new structure, it is often the site of angry animal-rights activists parading around it, carrying signs with "Down with research" or "Cuddle our animals."

This morning, a few of the peaceful marchers are yelling.

"Love pets! Save our horses!"

It is common knowledge among the citizenry that the foundation uses irradiated equine (horse) nerve tissue to treat patients with advanced terminal cancer. Oftentimes, a limousine drops off a courier carrying a box labeled, "Medical tissue, packed in dry ice" into the building.

Medical technologist Yolanda Ybarra grasps the crucifix hanging from her neck chain, utters a little prayer to the blessed Virgin Mary, and cautiously winds her way to work at the cancer center, keeping as much distance from the protesters as possible.

Yolanda, a lovely 5'4", twenty-eight-year-old woman, is of Mexican American heritage. Her high cheekbones and dark-brown, curly hair show off her emotions as they skim across her face. Her soft curves will entice any man, yet she presents a humble demeanor.

Once inside the building, she straightens her otherwise spotless uniform and enters the elevator to the laboratory on the third floor.

The laboratory itself is furnished with the latest and most advanced medical equipment for research—neat and most conducive to the scientists and technicians for doing this specialized, sophisticated work.

Ybarra finds the newly hired technologist, Elaine Franche, twenty-three, waiting for her, browsing through some pamphlets on a receiving table. Ybarra greets her.

"Ms. Franche, I'm Yolanda. I hope the rioters outside didn't bother you much."

Franche is young and away from home for the first time. She has a fresh Midwestern outlook on life and willing to learn—pretty, outgoing, very bright, and slender and shows her blonde, brown-eyed, medium height off well.

"I'm pleased to meet you, and please call me Elaine, Yolanda. No, the people outside didn't bother me at all. Oh, they are just animal nuts!"

"Yeah, they all start that way. Let me show you around and try to impress you with what we have here."

"No need to impress me, I can't believe I landed this job! The competition was so tough." Both laughed.

Smiling back, Yolanda said, "Hey, wait a minute. You come highly recommended by Mr. Westerman himself. It's good to have talented young people to round out our staff. This facility consistently shows one hundred percent cures for terminally ill cancer patients. We need you and people like you to keep it that way."

Franche and Ybarra inch their way through the busy laboratory. They reach a small corridor leading to a heavy door, which is locked. On the outside is a yellow board with a large, red "DANGER" and with a nuclear symbol painted on it.

Ybarra begins, "Everything we do begins behind that door. Only Dr. Davidson and his executive assistant, Mr. Westerman, have unlimited access inside."

"The Radiation Room?"

"Yes. We also call it the Rad or Red Room. The doctor and Mr. Westerman do the irradiation themselves. We have been told that the risk for even minimal radiation exposure is far too high for us."

"And what do they irradiate?"

"Special equine, or horse, nerve tissues, which are brought in by courier. After irradiation, they are emulsified in acetic acid and bovine serum albumin. By the time we get the material, it has already been emulsified."

"Well, I guess we won't be horsing around!" Both just laughed.

"Now that you've seen the entry to what most of us here call the inner sanctum, let's go back, and I'll show you what we do with the emulsified material."

They look at a modern centrifuge, which looks like a spaceship from Mars.

"I spin the emulsion at five thousand RPMs for five hours."

"Five hours?" Franche asks. "That's about as long as my flight from Milwaukee to Charleston!"

"What? I grew up in Waukesha! What do y'know, two badgers in Dixieland, huh? What a coincidence! Don't tell me you went to WCTI too."

"No, I attended the Medical College of Wisconsin. I am an M-COW alumna. It is close to where I grew up…in Elm Grove."

"Oh, the rich suburb. You must have been to see the Packers at Lambeau Field a few times too."

"Well, yes. My…my grandparents have season tickets. Grandpa used to take me to games whenever Grandma couldn't go."

"What do you know? That's all we need around here, a spoiled, rich cheese-head in Charleston! I… I never got to Green Bay, but I am a cheese-head myself. I watch the Packers on television every time I can. Now, where was I?"

"You are now five hours after the centrifuge stage," Franche answers.

"Okay," Ybarra continues. "I pipette out the precipitate and reconstitute it with exactly eighty cubic centimeters of liquid gelatin to make sixteen vials of five cubic centimeters each.

Then I place the vials into the freezer. They are kept frozen at minus seven degrees Fahrenheit, to be returned to room temperature right before they are injected into the patient."

Chatting and walking away from the centrifuge area down a corridor leading to another room, they hear soft music playing from the room.

"That's our lounge," Ybarra continues. "We have a microwave and all kinds of drinks and sandwiches available from a dispenser. Free coffee is available for us at all times. What do you say we take a short break there now?"

"This scares me. You can read my mind! Let's go," Franche agrees. "Coffee's on me."

Entering the room, they locate the coffee machine and the counter for cream and sweeteners.

The brightly lit room is well ventilated. Through the windows they can see the protesters outside, walking peacefully away from the building escorted by uniformed police.

The women find comfortable seating and resume their conversation.

Ybarra starts, "When I was at WCTI, we had a very handsome young professor of biochemistry and endocrinology, Bryan Lindbergh, MD, PhD. Oh, was he ever smooth and smart. Every girl in our class was in love with him!"

"I know Dr. Lindbergh, he taught at M-COW too. He just looks younger than his age. He has a wife and five children, all boys, in Menomonee Falls! I used to play with his boys when we were kids.

He and his wife are very active volunteers in the American Cancer Society. They'd go from high school to high school all over Milwaukee and Waukesha Counties, teaching students self-breast examination and lung cancer prevention. He and my father were medical school classmates at M-COW."

"Your dad is a doctor?"

"Yes, he is a surgeon practicing in Brookfield. He thinks a lot of Dr. Lindbergh too. After medical school, Dr. Lindbergh went to

Harvard to get his PhD in biochemistry. That is where he met his wife. Oh, what about you, Yolanda? You know a lot about me now."

"There's nothing much about me. My father and mother came from Mexico when I was just a baby. He worked for Harley-Davidson in Milwaukee until he retired a few years ago. We never did go anywhere except for a trip back to Guanajuato when my grandmother was very ill a long time ago."

"Guanajuato!" Franche said with excitement. "My parents love Guanajuato. One time they took me and my brother with them to Guanajuato. My brother and I explored underground Guanajuato until our feet ached. What beauty! Maybe someday you and I can go there, and you can show me where you were born."

"Oh, that'll be quite a trick. That was many years ago. Everything's changed now, Elaine. You can take me to a Packer game more realistically than me showing you my birthplace."

"Okay, Waukesha woman, how did you find your way down Dixie way?"

"That is a touching story,"

"I'm sorry, I didn't mean to pry."

"Don't be. I don't mind. Almost everybody here knows about it. Paul and I were classmates at WCTI. We were married a year after graduation."

Yolanda pauses briefly.

"At that time this foundation was actively recruiting medical technologists. We read about it in the *Wisconsin Medical Journal*, and we both applied. Would you believe, we both got accepted? Our first two years of marriage seemed as if made in heaven. I… I never realized a woman could enjoy such bliss and friendship with her husband."

Yolanda pauses again and continues.

"I never realized how much he wanted children"—Yolanda tears up—"We consulted a specialist at the medical university in town, and he diagnosed uterine fibroids, which is why I was never able to carry a pregnancy to term.

We started to stray away from each other gradually. Then one day I found a note pasted on our kitchen cupboard, telling me that he was leaving and asking me not to look for him."

"Please stop, Yolanda, I don't want to hear anymore." Franche holds Yolanda's hands.

"Okay, Elaine, okay, let's go to the fourth floor where we do the injections."

They leave the lounge to get to the elevators.

The fourth floor is compartmentalized into several semiprivate rooms where patients receive injections via slow drip or gradual push by syringes.

Patients are either lying down on single beds or comfortably relaxed on specially made chaise lounges.

On one of the bed lies an emaciated elderly woman whose abdomen is exposed just below her breasts.

"Some patients get their injections subcutaneously through their abdominal wall to avoid using their veins, which are sometimes difficult to find," Yolanda begins.

Franche notices that other patients are receiving oxygen by face masks. She gives Yolanda an inquisitive look.

"Yes, I'm glad you noticed that, Elaine. We have a lot of patients needing oxygen as they get their infusions."

They continue walking as Franche intently examines every step of the injection process.

Ybarra continues, "Five cc of the gelatinous solution are administered into the patient's tissues once a week for sixteen weeks."

"Why sixteen weeks?"

"Cancer cells take an average of eighty-five to one hundred and five days to double themselves. They don't do this all at the same time, or you'd see lumps double their size within split seconds. The gelatin permits the steady release of the anticancer factor for the eighty-five to one hundred and five days it takes the cells to multiply, catching them all."

"Why, that's amazing! What is this antineoplastic factor that is in the solutions?"

"Transforming factor gamma. It is a cytokine—a product of irradiated special equine nerve tissue. It reverses the DNA synthesis phase, or the most active growth phase of the multiplying cancer cells, killing them."

"But that seems so simple. How come no other laboratory has it?"

"That I cannot answer. The secret is hidden somewhere between the kind of equine nerve tissue and the irradiation process itself. Only Dr. Davidson and Mr. Westerman have that information. By the way, I appreciate that you are absorbing the information on what we do here. We encourage all our staff people to do that."

They reach the end of the room and pause close to the elevator doors. They step aside as people and loaded gurneys move in and out of the elevator.

Franche asks, "How many patients do you treat a year?"

"We see about over a hundred thousand patients a year. They come from all over the world."

"And what about your cure rate?"

"Roughly thirty to forty-five percent."

"That is outstanding, knowing that all of them have been considered incurable and terminal. But if the cytokine does reverse the DNA synthesis, would you think the cure rate should be much higher?"

"What an excellent question! Cancer cell differentiation has a lot to do with it. Well-differentiated cancer cells respond the least to any chemotherapy. So we only select patients with advanced, undifferentiated or most aggressive cancers.

Dr. Davidson, being a pathologist, reads all the slides himself. And even at that as you know, not all of them respond positively. So as we do not practice sex, race, or age discrimination, we do practice what you may say cellular discrimination."

"That makes sense, now where do you get the special equine nerve tissue? Is there a special horse farm associated with the foundation?"

With her right index finger covering her lips, Ybarra answered, "No one on the staff knows other than Davidson and Westerman. If that secret leaks out, it will be easy for the animal-rights people to destroy and ruin the foundation. The tissues come in via special couriers from, shall we say, sites unknown?"

"That makes sense. Are the treatments covered by insurance?"

"No. Our treatment is still waiting for approval by the FDA. It is still considered experimental."

As they walk the corridor between treatment compartments, a black baby lying in a crib with its head bandaged attracts Franche's attention through the glass window.

"Baby girl or boy?" she asks.

"I don't know its sex, but over the last five years we have restored the sight of eleven children with advanced retinoblastomas."

"Now that's almost miraculous! That cancer usually meant eye enucleation. If I may ask, what is the cost of treatment to the patients?"

"That's no secret. The foundation collects one hundred and twenty thousand dollars in escrow money before treatment starts."

"Wow, that's a lot of money."

"If the patient is one hundred percent cured and restored to good health, all money is retained. If there is evidence that even one, single cancer cell survived, all money is returned except for fifteen thousand dollars for nursing and administration costs and cytokine synthesis.

Oh yes, we do find an occasional patient who is allergic to the cytokine itself or any one of the preservatives. All patients are initially tested for allergic reaction before injection. In that case we retain only two hundred fifty dollars for the testing process. Let me take you down to the first floor. It's time you meet Dr. Davidson."

They get on an empty elevator to the first floor. Davidson's office occupies almost the entire east wing of the building.

Westerman's office is on the opposite wing. A number of small offices are occupied by clerks who are busily entering and retrieving data from computers at their desks. Nobody seems to notice the two of them walk past to knock on Dr. Davidson's office door.

A well-dressed young male assistant opens the door and courteously leads them in.

Looking directly at Franche, he says, "You must be the new hire. My name is Toby" and shakes her hand, acknowledging Yolanda with a nod.

"Dr. Davidson will be right with you."

The women sit down on extremely posh furniture while Franche scans the office.

On the wall, she notices Dr. Randolph Stern Davidson's medical diploma from Johns Hopkins University, a PhD diploma in cellular pathology from Heidelberg University, a certificate from the American Board of Internal Medicine and Fellowship in the International Society of Clinical Oncologists.

From a small door adjacent to his office Dr. Davidson, sixty-two, an impeccably dressed silver-haired gentleman, enters and greets the women with a warm smile.

Ybarra introduces Franche to Dr. Davidson.

Randolph Stern Davidson, MD, PhD, is well studied and often reclusive except for a few acquaintances. He really trusts no one. At five feet, ten inches tall and a little pudgy around the middle, he is soft-spoken, but with a hidden anger.

"Ms. Franche, I'm optimistic that you will find your work here challenging and fulfilling."

"There's no question, sir, Yolanda did a fantastic job of orienting me in the lab and injection rooms."

Davidson looks at Ybarra.

"Yolanda, did the marchers outside bother you?"

"Only a bit, sir."

"I want you, ladies, to be extra careful outside. Last week our security defused a packaged bomb."

"*Dios mio,*" Yolanda exclaimed. "Oh, I'm sorry."

"It's okay," Davidson continues. "Just be careful. Yolanda, be sure that you have Ms. Franche meet Westerman and get her own entry code and electronic card to the building."

"Of course, sir."

The women both leave Davidson's office. Yolanda introduces Elaine to several staff members as they walk back to the biochemistry laboratory.

"Elaine, would you mind taking care of things here next week Wednesday afternoon? I need to take my sister to her obstetrician. Juanita and her husband live in an apartment close to mine right here in town."

"Of course, how lucky for you to have family right here in the city with you."

CHAPTER 3

Glacier Medical Group
North Charleston, South Carolina

TWO FAMILY PRACTITIONERS, DR. PENDERGAST, age sixty, and Dr. Roller, age thirty-two, share an office suite on the fourth floor of a small building about ten miles north of the Davidson Foundation. Jules Pendergast, MD has been practicing as a general practitioner in the area for a long time. Six feet tall with sandy, blond hair and rugged good looks, he is adored by his patients. He is also living well above his means.

William Della Torre Roller, MD is 6'2", well-built, and with the looks of movie actor Gregory Peck. He possesses dark, curly, soft hair and a smile to charm anybody. His demeanor is gentle yet strong enough to carry weight.

Roller joined Pendergast the month before. He and Pendergast incorporated themselves into the Glacier Medical Group Inc.

Dr. Pendergast's busy practice has been there for almost fifteen years.

Roller's office is a storeroom in the suite, which has been recently converted to provide office space and two examining rooms. The odor of fresh paint on the walls still exists. Simple as it may look, it has all the equipment and materials, including refrigerator and freezer, that any physician's office needs. A single English ivy planter sits on a windowsill.

From the top floor of the building, one can barely see the tops of some trees at the Magnolia Plantation and Gardens.

A computer screen and printer are on Dr. Roller's desk as well as an unlit Warm Tobacco Pipe candle. Folded on one end of his desk is a copy of the *Wall Street Journal*. His name is carved on a very noticeable wooden sign at the front of his desk.

Roller's last patient in the afternoon waits for him in the consultation/examining room adjacent to his office.

"Dr. Roller, your last patient, Mrs. Devereau, is ready for you," his nurse, Mrs. Gretchen Martin, announces. She hands him the patient's medical chart.

Roller reads the record, pauses a bit, and follows Mrs. Martin into the room. He finds Mrs. Devereau already lying down on the examining table, ready for an abdominal examination. Two little girls are sitting on chairs next to her.

"Dr. Roller, I hope you don't mind that I brought my little girls with me today," Devereau asks.

"Oh no, Mrs. Devereau, your princesses are so pretty and so well-behaved."

"They came with me because they would like to listen to their baby brother's heartbeat."

"Of course."

Mrs. Martin exposes the patient's abdomen wider. Roller scans it with his stethoscope.

"Here, girls, your baby brother wants to talk to you!"

Two girls, age six and eight, eyes wide-open, almost shoved each other to get a chance to use the stethoscope as Roller plants its diaphragm firmly on one side of Devereau's abdomen.

Satisfied and smiling, the girls go back to their seats.

"Dr. Roller, thank you. You just made two princesses extremely happy. They would have had an older brother. But I miscarried my first baby, another boy, at four months. My husband was devastated. Dr. Pendergast and I just couldn't figure out how that happened."

"Well, I am sure your little princesses will have a little prince to spoil this time."

"We certainly hope so."

"I don't need to do any further examination right now. Your ultrasound, blood pressure, lab work, and baby follow-up are all in order."

Roller leaves the room.

Mrs. Martin assists the patient to get off the table.

He was ready to leave the office when Dr. Pendergast arrives.

"Bill, thank you very much for seeing Mrs. Devereau. That staff meeting at the hospital took so long! They've been arguing about adding on more beds for so long that I am ready to tell them to scrap the whole idea."

"No problem, Jules. If all our patients are like Mrs. Devereau, I would not mind working here for a very long time."

"Well, like any other clinic, there are a few you'd like to send elsewhere. I really came to tell you that I made an appointment for you to see a young fellow, Don Brighton. He is a financial planner. Reserve some time early in the afternoon next week for him, okay?"

"Thank you. I do appreciate that."

Donald Brighton, thirty, CPA, walks around the office as he waits for Roller to arrive. He is the junior partner of Brighton and Son Inc., Pension Services. His firm takes care of financial planning for several businessmen, lawyers, and physicians in the city, including Dr. Pendergast.

Pendergast has made the appointment for Mr. Brighton to see Dr. Roller for financial planning.

Roller greets Brighton with a smile as he enters his office. "I hope I didn't keep you waiting too long, Mr. Brighton. You are well recommended by Dr. Pendergast."

"Not at all, shall I call you Dr. Della Torre or Dr. Roller?" Brighton speaks as he looks back at the very noticeable sign on Roller's desk.

"Just call me Bill if you'll let me call you Don. I am expecting a long and harmonious relationship with your firm. Della Torre was my mother's maiden name," Roller continues talking as he sits on the chair behind his desk.

Brighton finds a comfortable chair across from him.

"Don, my mom was born in Brasilia in Brazil. She and my dad met in Rio at the Carnival. I was already in high school when I realized what they meant when they told me that my life started even before the samba ended."

"Well, Doc, you just convinced me to get on the very next plane to Rio de Janeiro!"

Both men laughed.

"Kidding aside, Bill, you should be able to put away at least eighteen percent of your gross—that is, before taxes—per year and build up your own IRA as soon as possible. Dr. Pendergast tells me that you are from San Diego."

"That's right. I graduated from UCSD and completed my family-practice residency at Mercy Hospital."

"What brings you all the way to the East Coast? You could have chosen a hundred other places in the country."

"Dr. Pendergast and the glamour of Dixie. I knew about Charleston from the number of medical meetings I've attended here, and when I found out that Dr. Pendergast was looking for someone new and talented to join him, through an ad on the *American Journal of Family Practice*, I gave him a call. The rest is history. He tells me that it will not be long before he thinks of retiring from practice."

"Do you think you'll miss San Diego?"

"Oh, I plan to visit my folks in Bonita, which is a suburb in San Diego, every once in a while."

"Bill, may I ask you a stupid question?"

"Fire away, Don."

"How were you able to escape from the lovely women in San Diego and stay single for so long?"

"Well, let us say I've had several encounters, but nothing worked out the way I wanted them to," Roller said with a smile.

"I'm not married either, Bill. Perhaps, the two of us can fly to Rio de Janeiro someday and dance the samba."

The voice of Roller's nurse on the intercom interrupts their conversation, "Dr. Roller, your first patient is ready."

"Bill, looks like the busy doctor life is taking over. We'll talk about your financial planning in a month, okay?"

Roller agrees, they shake hands, and Brighton departs the office.

Roller enters his simply, but efficiently equipped examining room and receives the patient's chart from his nurse, Mrs. Gretchen Martin.

He briefly pauses and politely acknowledges the presence of the two women as Mrs. Martin introduces him to the patient, Juanita Lemmer, twenty-one, and the patient's sister, Yolanda Ybarra.

Juanita is taller, by three inches, than Yolanda. She is lighter in color, with striking blue eyes. She is vivacious and often the life of any family party. She is married and settled down, but still first to speak up whatever comes to mind.

"Dr. Roller," Lemmer starts, "I already like you. You look much gentler than Dr. Pendergast."

Ybarra interrupts, "Please excuse my sister, Doctor, she can be outspoken at times."

"I assure you, ladies, that I will be as gentle as possible. Mrs. Lemmer, your chart records show that you are in your eighteenth week of gestation. I will do a thorough checkup and, if you like, request an ultrasound to see if you are carrying a prince or a princess inside."

Lemmer looks at Mrs. Martin and says, "Isn't he just sweet? Can I see Dr. Roller again next time?"

Roller answers, "I'd like that, but I'm only seeing you because Dr. Pendergast is out of town. He will be back in two weeks."

Mrs. Martin sets the examining table and prepares the patient for examination. While Roller examines Lemmer, Yolanda notices two certificates on the wall—a medical diploma from the University of California in San Diego and a certificate of completion of family-practice residency at Mercy Hospital, also in San Diego.

After the examination, Mrs. Martin helps Mrs. Lemmer from the exam table and has her sit on the chair next to the doctor's desk as Roller enters her information into the computer.

"Everything's fine," Roller assures Lemmer and Ybarra. "I expect a very smooth completion of your pregnancy to term."

"Thank you, Doctor," Lemmer acknowledges.

"I see that you went to medical school in San Diego," Yolanda says.

"Not only that but I was born in San Diego, grew up in San Diego, went to medical school, and completed my internship and residency in San Diego."

"Are you happy to finally get away from San Diego, Doctor? You didn't go far enough. You could have gone all the way to Maine," Lemmer teases.

"I love San Diego," Yolanda states. "My parents once took Juanita and me to San Diego to visit our uncle in Point Loma years ago. That was a fun trip. We saw Shamu, Old Town, and that old mission, Mission Basilica San Diego de Alcalá."

"I was baptized and confirmed there," Roller interrupts. "Ms. Ybarra, I see from your uniform that you work at the foundation, is that right?"

"Yes, Doctor, I am one of their senior technologists there. I've worked there for five years now."

"I've been told that the place is just short of fabulous."

"Would you like to see our place?" Ybarra invites.

"Sure would."

Ybarra then starts, "Let me give you a mental walk-through. The first floor is Administration. Second floor is experimental laboratory and equipment floor. The third floor is Biochemistry. That is where the irradiation room is. The fourth and fifth floors are all patient care and injection rooms."

"That sounds like a very well-planned medical facility. Now I can't wait to see it."

Roller hands Lemmer's health records to Mrs. Martin and flirts with Ybarra.

"Do I get a one-on-one tour, then, perhaps soon? I'm free Thursday afternoons."

"That can be easily arranged," Yolanda answers with a smile.

"Now, if that is not a date, I will be a monkey's uncle!" Lemmer interjects as everybody laughs and leaves the examining room.

"I will see you on Thursday afternoon, and may I call you Bill?"

"Certainly, Yolanda."

Chapter 4

DCRF, Charleston, South Carolina

Impeccably dressed in suit and tie, Roller punches the third-floor button on the elevator at the Davidson Cancer Research Foundation.

He exits the elevator and immediately looks for Yolanda's office.

To his surprise he sees both her and Elaine Franche walking toward him, engaged in a serious, animated conversation.

They almost don't see him coming.

Yolanda happily greets Bill and introduces him to Elaine.

"How about that, a doctor on time," Elaine teases.

"And starving," Bill adds. "If I were a cobra, I could've bitten you both before you saw me. Did you just lose a patient or something?"

"No, Doctor, we were discussing, and I was just overwhelmed by the mandatory slideshow on antitumor necrosis factor and carcinolysis that Mr. Westerman, Dr. Davidson's executive assistant, presented last night."

"Yes, Bill, every new hire has to attend that one-hour, rather in-depth session before they get their code and entry card into the building. As staff, we are allowed entry into the building after closing time, but I can tell you more about that later."

"Well then, let me change the atmosphere, Yolanda, and invite you to have dinner with me, we can get the tour going another time."

"Okay, let me get my jacket, and I am yours for the evening."

"Have fun, you two," Elaine smiles and walks away.

Bill gently puts his arm around Yolanda as they enter the elevator and leave the building.

"Yolanda, you've been here longer than I have been, can you suggest a nice, comfortable, relaxing restaurant in Charleston? And oh yeah, I love good Dixieland cuisine."

"I didn't think someone so hungry could be so picky," she says, smiling at him.

"Okay, let me think. Not too far from here is Shem Creek."

"That sounds farther than the moon."

"No, just a few miles out of town. Mr. Westerman talks about the restaurants there all the time. That's where the fishermen of Charleston do most of their shrimping. Juanita and I have been there, but not to eat. We just watched the shrimp boats going in and out of the harbor."

"Sounds good, colorful, and remember, I'm starved! Lead the way, but let me do the driving."

"It's about fifteen minutes away. We will drive north from the city and then go east across the Cooper River on the Ravenel Bridge to Shem Creek. I believe, Mr. Westerman grew up in Mount Pleasant where Shem Creek is."

"That's swell, you be the navigator."

"Okay."

CHAPTER 5

Shem Creek, South Carolina

BILL AND YOLANDA ARRIVE AT Shem Creek in no time. They drive around as Bill watches the shrimp boats move in and out of the harbor. Yolanda seems lost searching for something.

"Hey, enjoy the view, what the heck are you looking for?"

"LG Supper Club."

"Let's get this straight. I am maybe starting my practice here, and my name is not Howard Hughes."

"You're kidding, I thought all San Diegans were wealthy."

"Ha! I didn't come from La Jolla—"

Yolanda interrupts, "There it is, we almost missed it!"

They stop and make a sharp left turn to enter the parking lot of a rustic, but posh-looking building right on the creek.

"Yolanda, the next time, you drive, and I navigate, okay?"

Yolanda smirks. Roller scans the building as he parks the car.

"Wow, I've attended a lot of meetings in Charleston, but this place was not on the maps in any of the concierges."

"Not to worry, Bill, we will go dutch."

"That's not what I mean, sweetheart. I invited you, and I will treat, and that is final! I only hope they don't have Dom Pérignon on their menu!"

"Who is he?"

"Never mind."

A well-dressed maître d' greets the two and leads them to a comfortable seating for two, overlooking the creek.

He politely seats Yolanda, picks the white, laced napkin from her wineglass, and lays it on her lap.

With a slight bow, he tells them that their wine steward will soon be with them for their drink orders.

Bill quickly scans the wine list. He finds a chardonnay that is reasonably priced.

"Well, the wine prices are not so bad. At least."

Yolanda smiles. They look at the boats moving back and forth on the water.

"You've watched them before, Yolanda, which boats have shrimp, and which boats are going out shrimping?"

"That's easy. The boats sailing lower on the water are finished, and those sailing higher are still on their way."

"You are pulling my leg. Were you ever on a shrimp boat before?"

"Never, but that seems like a very logical answer."

"To tell you the truth, I was in the naval reserve for a few years on Coronado."

"Does that make you a shrimp boat expert?"

Before Bill can answer, their wine steward arrives, and with Yolanda's approval, he selects a bottle of chardonnay from Tobin James Winery in Paso Robles, California.

"Excellent choice, sir. That will go well with any of the seafood we serve here." The steward leaves.

"You impressed the steward and me. Are you a wine expert?"

"No, I attended a meeting at UCLA once, and the concierge at the hotel featured a wine-tasting tour in Paso Robles, which is about two hundred miles north of LA. It took us almost all morning to get there and almost all afternoon to get back, but the wine tasting was fantastic. I ended up coming home with several bottles of really good wine. One of them is this chardonnay. I recognized it."

"What is a wine-tasting tour like?"

"Oh, you poor girl, perhaps, someday I can take you on a tour of as many wineries as can be found in California."

Their waiter arrives.

"Good afternoon, ma'am, sir, would you like to know about our specials today?"

"No," Bill answers. "I think we've made up our minds already."

"I'll take your shrimp creole," Yolanda answers.

"And I'll have the blackened redfish."

"Sir, the fish is quite spicy."

"I come from Southern California, I can handle that."

"He will chase it down with chardonnay and iced water."

The waiter smiles and leaves.

"You seem to know what this blackened redfish is all about."

"Spicy or not, it should really be good. I had that in Pensacola, Florida, at Knife and Fork School when I joined the naval reserves."

Yolanda starts laughing.

"Knife and fork. Did they teach you how to row a boat too?"

"Not unless you are going to be in a submarine. Kidding aside, Knife and Fork School is a series of introductory sessions given to new officers on the customs and traditions of the United States Navy, which is patterned after the British Navy."

"Okay, sailor, I can't wait to see you handle that fish dish."

The waiter arrives and places their food on the table.

"Oh, our selections smell wonderful, thank you!"

Bill looks at the waiter appreciatively.

"Thank you, sir."

The waiter bows his head politely and leaves.

The two make the sign of the cross and proceed to enjoy their dinner.

"Yolanda, something truly bugs me. You and Elaine were in a very serious conversation earlier today."

"We were just going over the technical information that she learned at the session last night. She was asking me about how transforming factor gamma is released from irradiated equine nerve tissue."

"Transforming factor what?"

"Gamma."

"That's Greek to me."

"Latin."

"I know, but whatever it is, I've not read about it in any of the books or journals or even from the available Internet. And what does this transforming factor gamma do?"

"It reverses the DNA synthesis phase of a rapidly growing cancer cell, the faster the cell grows, the more effectively this cytokine kills it."

"You mean it works like an antitumor necrosis factor, or TNF."

"I don't know about TNF, but that's what cytokine is supposed to do."

"And you get this cytokine by just nuking certain horse nerve tissues?"

"Yes."

"Boy, I'll accept that, but with reservations although one really cannot fight success. I saw that movie with Forrest Trask and the Academy Awards presentation on TV."

"What movie?"

"*Space Station Zulu*. I thought everybody had seen that one. Trask spoke very highly of Dr. Davidson and the foundation. He said that he was dying from cancer, and his treatment from your foundation cured him completely. Now you know that you are really working for a most elite institution. Probably more famous than the Mayo Clinic in Minnesota."

"Then you think I should get paid better than what I'm getting?"

"I'd certainly holler, scream, and make a scene!"

The two finish their dinner and scan the dessert menu.

"This cream puff looks really good," Yolanda suggests.

"No, I'll go for the crème brûlée."

"Back in Wisconsin—"

Bill interrupts.

"I was really going to ask about you, please go on."

"Well, back in Wisconsin my ex and I used to go to the State Fair in Milwaukee just to eat and enjoy the cream puffs they served there."

"Your ex?"

"I might as well tell you more about me."

"Oh, please."

"I was born in Guanajuato, Mexico."

"How far is that from Tijuana?"

"A long, long way. My parents came to this country when I was a baby and settled in Waukesha, Wisconsin. I grew up there, went to high school there and college at WCTI."

"WCTI?"

"Waukesha County Technical College. Paul and I were married right after we finished college. He was my classmate. We both sent our applications to work at Davidson Cancer Research Foundation and, fortunately, got accepted together. To make a long story short, he wanted children, and I could not provide that for him because I have fibroid uterus. He left me, and that was that!"

"Oh gee, I'm awfully sorry."

"Please don't be. I think it was the best for the both of us."

"Do you miss Wisconsin?"

"A lot of times, but my younger sister, whom you met, and her husband are here living in an apartment close to mine. I don't know how long they will be here. Her husband, Jerry, is on active duty, working at the naval base near here. What about you, do you miss San Diego?"

"It's too early to tell. If I get busy, and I hope I will, I will probably miss San Diego less. Although I do plan to visit my parents there periodically."

"Bill, I notice that you are Catholic."

"Is it that obvious?"

"You made the sign of the cross at the same time I did just before we ate."

"I did not just grow up in San Diego. Not only was I baptized and confirmed at the Mission Basilica San Diego de Alcala, but also my parents exchanged their vows there."

"Oh, how I'd like to visit those missions I've read about in California."

"Have no fear, perhaps, someday we will just do that."

After their dinner the two walk out unto the rustic balcony of the restaurant and admire the beauty of the nature surrounding them. The soft, haunting sound of the "Song of Hawaii" accompanies the couple as they walk. Bill looks into Yolanda's eyes and asks,

"Yolanda, would you mind having dinner with me again sometime soon?"

"Oh, would I love that, but before we go any further and this hand-holding becomes serious, remember what I told you about my condition at dinner tonight?"

"Yolanda, millions of children all over the world need loving parents and... I hope you know what I'm driving at."

She takes his hand, and they walk in the soft dusk of the evening to the car.

CHAPTER 6

Wynn Las Vegas

THE EVENING IS ALIVE AND noisy in the brightly lit and opulent main floor of the Wynn Las Vegas. Gamblers are practically yelling at one another just to overpower the sound of music and the clanging of bells.

But in the spacious suite of Davros Westerman on the tenth floor, fifty physicians are quietly conversing with one another. Davros, or Dave, Westerman and Davidson own the foundation together.

Davidson handles all their medical aspects while Westerman keeps the books and assures that the foundation remains solvent. A biologist and with a master's degree in business administration, he has the distinguished look.

He sports a classic, perfect beard making him appear more dapper. Standing a stately six feet and in shape from daily workouts, his good looks have always opened doors for him: a political guy to go to get things done his way and a six-figure income to grease any wheels—underhanded in many ways.

The physicians all wear Davidson Cancer Research Foundation tags with their names, the city and state they are from in easily readable print. Uniformed waiters and waitresses provide them with drinks and an unending flow of hors d'oeuvres. Soon Davidson and Westerman are with them, greeting everyone with warm handshakes.

All settle down and are comfortably seated as Davidson takes the podium.

Westerman assures that the door is closed and the servers have all been excused and the room is secure. Then he takes one of the seats up front.

Davidson starts.

"Good evening, ladies and gentlemen. Thank you all for being here tonight. Mr. Westerman and I"—he glances at Westerman, who rises and smiles at the seated crowd—"hope that you enjoyed your flight here and are enjoying your stay in Las Vegas. We have arranged to give you and your better halves a dinner and show after this brief meeting."

The doctors whistle and applaud.

"The foundation is doing well right now, but I, for one, am not sure how long we can keep this up. Laboratories in Europe and the Far East are actively trying to synthesize prototensin. We desperately need more members to join our group."

One of the attendees, Dr. Archibald Frankle, raises his hand. Archibald O. Frankle, MS, MD acts as spokesman and leader of this select group of physicians that keeps the foundation going with a seemingly unending supply of hypothalami for prototensin extraction. He is gifted with a knack to make people instantly like him, trust him, and follow his lead.

"Yes, Arch," Davidson acknowledges.

"Randy, several members of our group had asked me to bring this matter up to you. Family practitioners around the country are staying away from obstetrics as you know. We have to be quite selective approaching physicians we talk to. We are left with recruiting obstetricians who are reluctant to even consider our idea. We are now trying to go into abortion clinics, but those folks are unreliable. Perhaps, if you raise our remuneration to, say, twenty grand each hypothalamus, it might be a bit easier."

"Wait a minute, Arch, sixty grand for a set of four is not pocket change, realizing that this is all tax-free. Thanks to Davros Westerman. We are able to absorb all tax implications mainly through our philanthropic work."

Westerman rises and politely motions Davidson that he wants the floor. Davidson gives him a nod.

"Folks, our real problem is RU-486. We all know that alone, it is almost ninety-five percent effective in terminating pregnancies. We need not only new members, but also new members who can be empathic enough to convince their women patients to carry their first-term pregnancies up to about the time that prototensin can be harvested, and you all know what I mean.

May I remind you all too that the hypothalami need to be frozen within two hours of harvest time. Kept frozen, the prototensin will remain effective for up to eight months until it is reconstituted at the center. This should give you enough time to get a set of four, depending on the number of pregnant women you see in your clinics."

Davidson added, "Isn't that really odd, scientists all over the world can come up with all kinds of ways to terminate pregnancies, and not a single one of them, so far, can come up with a truly effective way of killing cancer cells?"

Westerman walks to the door, opens it, and asks the waiters and waitresses to come back and to continue serving food and drinks.

CHAPTER 7

Pathology Department
Saint Bonaventure Hospital

DRESSED IN SURGICAL GOWNS, DR. Jules Pendergast and pathologist Dr. Eric Rieser gaze intently at a miscarried male fetus lying on a table at the morgue adjacent to St. Bonaventure Hospital in Downtown Charleston. The placenta has been carefully dissected out.

"Dr. Rieser, did you do a full autopsy on this fetus? I am really at a loss. The mother carried her pregnancy so well that I expected a full-term delivery."

"Perhaps, the fetus itself is defective, and that is why I performed a full examination including its brain tissue. We will have to wait until the slides are ready for a more detailed assessment, Dr. Pendergast."

"Please do that." Rieser leaves the room while Pendergast continues to look at the tiny male fetus on the table.

When Rieser is out of sight, Pendergast takes a small metallic spoon out of a hidden plastic container from his pocket, scoops a small piece of brain tissue, places it securely inside a glass vial, and hurriedly leaves the room. Outside he meets Rieser, who is returning to the room.

"Dr. Rieser, please let me know what your final diagnosis will be. I will be most interested."

"Of course, Doctor."

CHAPTER 8

Roller's Apartment
North Charleston, South Carolina

THE GARDEN APARTMENT BUILDING COMPLEX is richly landscaped with flowering azaleas and magnolia trees. On the fourth floor is Apartment 446, which Bill Roller occupies. The single-bedroom flat is a bit larger than an efficiency with kitchen, living room, study room, and full bath. Bill has just brushed his teeth and is ready to leave for his office as he watches the weather report on television. His phone rings.

"Bill, good morning, this is Yolanda."

He turns the sound down on the TV.

"How are you, Yolanda, did you sleep well last night?"

"No, not quite so."

"What happened?"

"Bill, Juanita had a miscarriage."

"Oh no! She was doing so well when I saw her, and I expected her pregnancy to go to term."

"It's so terrible, she is crying and beside herself. She and Jerry are right here with me. I am trying to soothe their pain somehow."

Juanita's husband, Jerry, twenty-four, is a warrant officer in the United States Navy. He is a career navy man. It was his dream as a young man. Standing a good 6'4" tall, he has a slender physique, a joyful exterior, the trust of his men, and the love of his life.

"I really don't know what to say, Yolanda. The only time I saw her was when Pendergast was out of town. It's just too bad. That used to happen more frequently years ago, but with advances in modern medicine, it has become less and less frequent."

"I just wanted to let you know."

"I'm really sorry for Juanita."

"Oh, by the way, when would you like me to take you around our facility?"

"How about Friday afternoon, Yolanda? Then we can go back to that lovely place in Shem Creek for dinner."

"Oh, and about Shem Creek, Mr. Westerman grew up in Mount Pleasant, the town where the creek is located. He suggested another place we can explore."

"Oh yeah? LG's would be tough to beat, but it will be worth a try."

"He tells me that most of Charleston's musicians, architects, and other artists dine there. Their menu includes good Southern recipes, and they have beer on tap from all over the world."

"Do you have the name?"

"Yes, Patti's."

"Then it's a date. Give my condolences to Jerry and Juanita, please."

They were ready to leave her apartment when her phone rings.

"Yolanda, Bill here. Mom called right after you hung up. Cancel our Friday date at the center. I need to fly back to San Diego ASAP. My dad had a heart attack last night. He is at the hospital right now, getting prepped for an angiogram. I need to sign my patients out to Pendergast. Fortunately, I don't have a lot of them yet. I'll let you know as soon as I get there."

"Oh my good lord, Bill, do you need a ride to the airport?"

"No, I'd rather drive myself and leave my car at the airport. And you will be the first to know when I get back."

"Be safe, Bill, and take care. I'll keep you and your family in my prayers."

Juanita notices Yolanda's concerned look. "Is there anything wrong?"

"Yeah, Bill's dad had a heart attack in San Diego. He'll be flying there now."

"*Madre mía*, I hope it is easily fixable?"

"He is getting an angiogram, and they will see. I hope he can get by without an open-heart."

"Hey, sis, you and Dr. Roller seem to be seeing more and more of each other," Juanita teases Yolanda.

"From what I gather, he is a hell of a lot better than Paul," Jerry quickly agrees. "I'd like to meet him."

"Oh, honey," Juanita continues as she looks at her husband, "to begin with, he has the looks of Gregory Peck!"

"Oh my god, what a formidable brother-in-law he will be!"

"C'mon, you two,"—Yolanda blushes—"don't jump to conclusions so quickly. For now, Bill is just a friend."

"Friend, my foot, never have I seen you so excited over a fellow in all my life! Jerry, take me home, please."

They all prepare to leave.

"Will do, honey, let's get going."

CHAPTER 9

DCRF
Charleston

WEEKS LATER AT THE DAVIDSON Cancer Research Foundation, animal laboratory caretakers, headed by Manny Timmerman, thirty-eight, clean out animal debris and reload feeding trays constantly. Housed in individual cages, rats, mice, and guinea pigs are kept meticulously clean and properly cared for.

Timmerman is sort of a mousy man. He is laid-back and a huge animal lover.

He moves through the labs, almost a shadow figure. He is overweight with his stubby beard contrasting his neat, clean white work clothes. He hardly notices Bill and Yolanda come into the room.

Dressed in crisp, clean white smocks with DCRF imprinted on their pockets, Bill and Yolanda move about slowly, examining the immaculately clean facility.

"Bill, I really appreciated your keeping me informed about your dad's progress while he was in the hospital."

"Well, as I told you before, his heart attack was considered mild, and all he needed was a stent in his left anterior descending coronary artery. He stayed at home for a week and went right back to work."

"I never asked you before, what does your dad do?"

"He is a surgeon in Bonita, but let us finish this tour, and I'll tell you more about my family at dinner tonight."

"Okay, there really isn't much to see down here after you've seen the biochemistry lab. I have the feeling that they are trying to find a way to clone these animals and synthesize that cytokine somehow. We have rats, mice, and guinea pigs. You didn't expect to see horses here, or did you?"

"That would have been a big surprise."

"I'm really intrigued with transforming factor gamma, Yolanda, how whatever that is can be extracted by irradiating nerve tissue."

"If everything in medicine is explainable, Bill, then why doesn't the acid in a vulture's stomach, which is stronger than the acid in your car battery, not digest the bird's stomach itself?"

"I don't know, Yolanda, but I know that my stomach can handle anything that Patti's restaurant at Shem Creek has listed on their menu. As long as I can chase it down with a good beer."

"Do you want me to navigate again, or is it my turn to drive?"

"No, I'll do the driving. I like driving."

"Okay, oh, but before I forget, Bill, did Dr. Pendergast tell you anything about Juanita's baby boy? He told her that he requested a full autopsy on him."

"All Pendergast told me was that he was as flabbergasted as I was about the miscarriage. He knew that I saw Juanita when he was out of town."

CHAPTER 10

Shem Creek, South Carolina

THIS TIME THE DRIVE TO Shem Creek goes smoother than silk. They get to Patti's as if they have dined there before. The atmosphere at Patti's is much more relaxed compared to LG's, but the decor is just as rustic. On the wall are paintings depicting battles fought during the Civil War.

One of them is an old painting of Fort Sumter. A neatly dressed black waitress meets them at the door as Bill looks intently at the painting of Fort Sumter.

"Table for two, please," Yolanda tells the waitress.

"Give me about five minutes, please. Our waiting lounge is over there."

She answers and points in the direction of the lounge. Waiting in the lounge, Yolanda is surprised to see a familiar face.

The man sees Yolanda and rises from his seat.

"Yolanda, what a surprise!"

"Rodger Eastwood, what a delight to see you here," Yolanda responds as she notices the lady seated next to Rodger.

"Yolanda, this is my wife, Adriane."

"And this is my friend, Dr. Bill Roller."

The four greet one another and exchange pleasantries.

"Bill, Rodger and I are in the choir at Immaculate Heart of Mary Church in town."

"She is our lead soloist," Rodger added.

"And Rodger carries the bass, he is our own Bing Crosby."

As the four consider sitting together, the waitress comes in and announces, "Your table is ready, Mr. Eastwood."

"Miss, can you find us a table for four?" Rodger asks as he looks to check with Bill, who nods.

"It'll be just a few more minutes, sir."

"Oh, that will be great," Bill agrees as he smiles at Yolanda.

"Rodger," Bill asks. "Since it looks like you two have eaten here before, is the food really, really good here?"

"Definitely, their fried green tomatoes are to die for. Let's all share an order for hors d'oeuvres."

"Hmm, do they fry okra too?"

"No, Yankee, you have to go to New Orleans for that, where they use okra with their rabbit stew. Yolanda, you need to really orient Bill to Southern-style cooking. To me and Adriane it is the best in the country."

"You bet, Rodger, I will certainly do my best." They continue their animated conversation as the waitress returns and announces, "Table for four ready for Mr. Eastwood."

They follow her inside the dining room to a roomy table for four.

"I'll be back to take your order. Here is our beer selection. Today we are featuring dark Bavarian beer from Germany."

"Do you have Czech pilsner?" Bill asks very quickly.

"Of course, sir."

"Whoa, Bill, you must know your beers!"

"Rodger, part of my heritage is Bohemian. My dad always told my brother and me that our great-grandparents lived in a town called Knappendorf, somewhere between Germany and Czechoslovakia. I don't think he had been there before himself, but he always asked for Czech pilsner whenever our family ate out together."

"Maybe I'll have that too, then," Adriane agrees and tells the waitress, "Four large steins of Czech pilsner, please!"

"Jawohl, it is October anyway," Yolanda says as the waitress walks away from their table.

"So, Bill, where is your practice?"

"I do family medicine with Dr. Pendergast at the Glacier Medical Group in North Charleston, Rodger."

"Oh, I thought you might be associated with the Davidson Foundation."

"No, but I'm also on the staff at St. Bonaventure Hospital."

"I'm a licensed practical nurse, and I used to work at St. Bonaventure too," Adriane adds.

"Well, with all three of you in the medical profession, I am the outsider here," Rodger states. "I asked because I know that Yolanda is employed by the foundation."

"We have only one MD at the foundation." Yolanda looks at Rodger and continues, "All the rest of us are medical technologists and biologists plus supporting staff such as animal caretakers."

Their steins of pilsner arrive, and another waitress comes to take their order.

"Anything but fried green tomatoes for me," Bill starts.

"Oh, c'mon, Bill, be a reb! It's delicious," Rodger insists.

"Okay, if you can enjoy pilsner, I might as well get used to Southern cooking. I expect to be here in Charleston for a long time."

"Wait, you guys," Yolanda says, "someday I'll have us four to my apartment, and I will whip up delicious Northern Mexican cuisine for you."

"Where the heck is Northern Mexico?" Adriane asks.

"Waukesha, Wisconsin," Yolanda responds. They all laugh and place their meal orders to the waiting waitress, who is likewise amused.

As they enjoy their meals and drinks, Bill starts, "Do you two have children?"

"Four healthy boys," Adriane boasts.

"We would have had a basketball team had Adriane not miscarried our oldest son."

"Oh, I'm so sorry."

"Bill, we worked so hard and carefully with our obstetrician. She even took very special vitamin pills when she was four or five months pregnant, but...even our doctor was surprised when she miscarried our baby."

"What can I say? Things do happen in medicine that cannot be explained no matter how you try. Rodger, since you said that you are not in medicine, what is your field of specialization in Charleston?"

"Rodger is an architect associated with the Bradford Group," Adriane interrupts.

"As a matter of fact, we did the planning for the construction of the Davidson Cancer Foundation's building. I spent a lot of time there when the building was going up."

"It is a marvelous work of construction," Yolanda adds. "My workplace is in the biochemistry department, which is on the third floor. That is really the hub of our research activity. My team of technologists prepares the solutions that we use to administer to the patients—that is, after the nerve tissue has been irradiated."

"Do you send these tissues out for irradiation first?"

"No, Rodger, we do the irradiating right there in a separate locked room on the third floor."

"You look shocked, Rodger," Bill says.

"Funny, but I don't remember any of the rooms in the entire building, being constructed for radiation purposes."

"There is a big, red door with radiation warning signs painted on the outside," Yolanda assures Rodger. "Only Dr. Davidson and his executive assistant, Mr. Westerman, have the keys for the door. We are not allowed to even get close to the door."

"I don't remember any of the rooms there fitting the code for radiation purposes, like lead-shielded walls and doors. The warning signs will only prevent people from entering the room, but it will not stop radiation from leaking out and eventually nuking all of you."

Rodger responds with a smile. "Then there is something definitely not quite right taking place in that room, and whatever it is, it is not irradiation."

"You are damn right, Rodger."

"Or shielding and radiation protection had been added after the building was fully constructed," Rodger assures Bill and Yolanda.

"I doubt that," Yolanda says. "I've seen them enter and leave the room, and that door doesn't look really thick nor heavy to me."

"Our office still has the building plan in storage, and so does the county office, if you two care to look at it?"

"We might just do that, Rodger," Bill concludes and notices something. "What is that funny-looking white thing on your plate, Adriane?"

"Sweetbread, Bill, and I love it. Our neighbor lady makes it regularly."

"Bill, what is sweetbread?"

"Calf pancreas, Yolanda," Bill answers rather quickly. "I only know that because I ran into Dr. Pendergast at the Palm Street Butcher Shop one time when I was looking for a nice fillet. I sort of surprised him. The butcher was just handing him that rather pricey selection when he saw me. He told me what it was and told me that his wife, Lorena, does an absolutely fantastic job of preparing sweetbread."

After dinner and dessert, the four exchange pleasantries. They continue to admire the beauty of the environment around them for a while and then proceed to the parking lot to their cars.

"It's interesting, what Rodger told us, Yolanda, how can you guys irradiate tissue in a room without adequate radiation protection?"

"Bill, both Davidson and Westerman always wear those radiation counter tags on their smocks every time they go into the room."

"For interest's sake, do you think you can borrow them for me to satisfy my curiosity?"

"Quite easily, they are there all the time. I'll just pick them up when they are away, which happens frequently."

"Okay, give them to me, and I'll have them read by X-ray techs at the hospital."

"Will do."

Holding hands, Bill and Yolanda walk ever so slowly to their car.

CHAPTER 11

DCRF, Charleston, South Carolina

THE NEXT MORNING AS ELAINE and Yolanda work, spinning vials of emulsified solutions in the centrifuge at the biochemistry laboratory, Davidson and Westerman approach the two. Looking at Ybarra, Davidson asks, "Have you been checking and double-checking all our emulsified specimens?"

"Yes, sir," Yolanda answers. "Is there a problem?"

"One set of four emulsified solutions is missing."

"*Dios mio*, I don't know how it could have been misplaced. We check and cross-check them all with the appropriate labeling each and every time. We will certainly find the missing vials for you."

"Please do that." Westerman walks away with Davidson, angrily shaking his head.

CHAPTER 12

Athletic Men's Club
Charleston, South Carolina

WEEKS LATER, IN A SMALL meeting room at a posh men's athletic club just outside of the city, Dr. Davidson, Dr. Archibald Frankle, and Davros Westerman engage themselves in a friendly, but serious conversation.

"Thank you for flying down and coming to meet with us today, Arch, but this is damn serious," Davidson starts. "Betrayal and treachery are two acts I will not abide with the group.

I, for one, have always done my part in remunerating all the members of the group for all the hypothalami we receive as agreed upon in our unwritten contracts. One of our members, Jules Pendergast, cheated by substituting sweetbread for the fourth specimen."

"Good lord, what was he trying to do?" Frankle answers.

"Whatever it was, it cannot be tolerated. It took us a hell of a long time, and we spent a lot of money to get this figured out. On top of that, we lost a very important Japanese client, who could well have been an excellent protégé for public advertising in the Far East," Davidson continues.

"His new partner, Dr. Roller, wouldn't know anything about this, would he, Randy?" Westerman directs his question to Dr. Davidson.

"Hell no! All he knows about our treatment is the transforming factor gamma that we have been feeding everybody at the foundation."

"Good, then perhaps, you can even recruit him to join the group through Pendergast and his wife, Lorena, who happens to be your cousin, I know."

"Ha, fat chance! Right now I'm so upset at that swindler, I could castrate him with my bare hands!"

"Whoa, Randy, that's my job," Frankle claims. "As head of the group I will do the punishing and the...that castration as needed."

"Roller will be an excellent recruit, Arch," Westerman says. "He is new, very personable, great-looking guy, single and openly interested in dating our senior tech, Yolanda Ybarra, who is also single. I know that because I just told Yolanda about this wonderful restaurant in Shem Creek that she and Roller were going to try a couple of days ago."

"Have you met him, Randy?" Frankle asks.

"No, but I've seen him with our technicians Yolanda Ybarra and Elaine Franche at the foundation. And I do agree with everything Dave said. Only, he is still new in the area. We need to give him time, develop his own practice. Give him a couple of years or so. And, hopefully, the scientists here and abroad will not have synthesized prototensin by then..."

"And that he does not get swayed to stay out of obstetrics by his modern cospecialists," Westerman finishes Davidson's statement.

"Yep, let's get some dinner, I'm starved," Frankle concludes, and the three make their way to the dining room.

CHAPTER 13

Basement, St. Bonaventure Hospital Charleston, South Carolina

MONTHS LATER THE MEDICAL STAFF presents a drug fair at St. Bonaventure's Hospital. Several pharmaceutical companies have set up separate display stands full of drug samples, sales gimmicks, and pamphlets.

Drug representatives entice physicians, nurses, and other staff members to pick out and take whatever they please in addition to asking questions on new pharmaceuticals and the instruments on display.

They serve coffee, doughnuts, and other goodies. All enjoy lively conversations. Dr. Pendergast leafs through one of the latest publications on obstetrics under the watchful eyes of a salesman.

"Dr. Pendergast, does that journal have the information you are looking for?" the salesman asks and points to another stack of papers. "These just came in from the Mayo Clinic."

"No, Stan, I'm looking for the latest on cytokines in obstetrics."

"I'm sure it's in there if it has been published, Doctor. These are our latest."

A man in a three-piece suit, carrying a thin walking stick and wearing a name tag labeled Fowler Schmidt, §MŒRKLE PHARMACEUTICALS§, shadows Pendergast's every move. He is 5'6" tall, balding, and appears to have an ego much larger than his physical figure.

He jabs Pendergast on the back of his left leg with the walking stick and stealthily disappears into the crowd of staff and drug representatives viewing the exhibits. Pendergast reacts briefly by scratching his calf area. He scans other books, then mingles, and enjoys the abundant goodies offered by the exhibitors with the other sales personnel and guests.

Dr. Pendergast drives his late model Jaguar Vanden Plas home after the hospital drug fair rather disappointedly because of not finding what he was specifically looking for from the latest publications. He grabs his chest, grimaces with pain, and slumps onto the steering wheel.

The car continues to drive aimlessly through traffic, narrowly missing other vehicles, and ultimately hits a lamppost.

The airbag inflates and pushes Pendergast's body away from the steering wheel. Other drivers stop their cars and view Pendergast's lifeless body pressed by the airbag into the seat.

CHAPTER 14

Cemetery

AZALEAS STILL BLOOM UNDER MAGNIFICENT magnolia trees inside the gated, well-manicured All Saints Cemetery just outside the city limits. Bill and Yolanda are part of a circle of mourners attending Dr. Pendergast's interment. Pendergast's widow, Lorena, hangs on to Dr. Davidson, her cousin, as a minister performs the rites of a Christian burial.

Lorena Pendergast, fifty-nine, is soft-spoken, very well put together, and involved in country club and social whirl. Green eyes and graying hair give her an air of trustworthiness. Today she is dressed all in upscale black. Fowler Schmidt stands behind Lorena and watches the conduct of the family at the ritual. He walks away with the crowd as the service ends.

Davidson holds on to Lorena and motions Bill and Yolanda to stay behind as the other people walk around them to their cars.

"Yolanda, Dr. Roller." He looks at Bill rather quizzically. Bill nods. "Perhaps, Jules never got the chance to introduce you to his wife, this is Lorena, his widow. Lorena, if you have not yet met these wonderful people, meet Dr. William Roller, Jules's partner, and Ms. Yolanda Ybarra, our senior tech at the foundation."

"Oh, I am so glad to meet you two finally. And please call me Lorena. Jules has spoken about the two of you often. It is really my fault that I have not met you, Dr. Roller. It's just that his passing was so sudden. He never drank to excess, never smoked, and had a tread-mill test only two months ago."

"Please, Mrs. Pendergast, or Lorena, don't blame yourself. I could have also asked Jules to have me meet his loving wife."

"Let us now do something about that," Lorena replies. "After I have had some recovery time—perhaps, a couple of weeks or so—maybe then I can have you and Yolanda to my home for dinner?"

"That will be wonderful. Tell us what Bill and I can bring with us to help you, Lorena," Yolanda says with a soft smile.

They all politely exchange goodbyes and leave.

Driving home, Yolanda looks back at the cemetery and says, "That cemetery is really as beautiful as the other techs at the foundation have described it."

"Oh, is that where all your failures at the foundation go to be buried? They'll probably have to make it bigger. As for me, I'd rather be cremated."

"A good-looking fellow like you? Your friends won't get the chance to look at your handsome face at the viewing."

"Yolanda, have you been to Baton Rouge, Louisiana?"

"No."

"I went to New Orleans for a meeting during my residency, and one of the hotel tours I took was a trip to the Bayou area. We passed by a cemetery where all burials are aboveground. The tour guide told us that you cannot dig for underground burial because of water, which could, in time, sweep away the corpses."

"Now I know why you want to be cremated. We can just fling your ashes away and add you to our air pollution problem."

"Kidding aside, Yolanda, I got the final readings on the radiation counters that you borrowed from Davidson's and Westerman's smocks, and guess what?"

"What?"

"They both read zeros."

"Then it's either you guys at the hospital don't know how to count, or there is absolutely no radiation going on in that room."

"They are very careful at the hospital and would not risk not knowing their exposure indices."

"Oh well, right now, Bill, I'll have to figure out what we can bring with us to Lorena's dinner."

"Perhaps, a good example of what you savor there in Wisconsin?"

"There is another thing you don't know about me."

"What?"

"I am one Hispanic who loves Italian cooking."

"And so do I."

"Now, please don't tell me that you just attended another of those damn meetings, this time in Rome."

"No, in Moscow."

"You've been to Russia too?"

"No, Moscow, Indiana."

"I tell you what, buddy boy, with Pendergast gone, Magnolia Park is probably the farthest away that you can go to if ever you get a break from seeing all his patients and yours."

"Then I'll follow the lead I get from my modern colleagues and stay away from OB. That'll take care of a lot of night calls."

CHAPTER 15

Roller's Office

DR. PENDERGAST'S DEATH TAKES A toll on Roller's leisure time as more and more names are listed on his patients' roster. He finds less and less time to call Yolanda even for a short visit. This afternoon is a little different. He sees a familiar name written on the chart of his next patient. He enters the door; two women and his nurse greet him.

"Juanita, Yolanda, great to see you both!"

"Bill, if the only way I can have a little time with you is to make an appointment, then I'll do it." Yolanda smirks and turns to leave Juanita with the doctor and his nurse.

"I'm sorry, Yolanda, please stay. I've really not been able to balance my clinic time yet."

"I agree to that," Mrs. Martin adds. "It's been like Grand Central Station here since Dr. Pendergast passed away. And Dr. Roller has attended more nighttime deliveries to boot."

"You guys," Juanita interrupts, "I am the patient here, I need all your attention."

"Yes, Juanita, what can I do for you?" Roller asks.

"I think I'm pregnant again. I haven't had a period for almost two months, and I feel it in my system that maybe I'm carrying a little person," Juanita says and points to her belly.

"That's absolutely good news. I'll check you out, get a urine sample, and let us see."

"May I remind you, Dr. Roller," Yolanda speaks, "we talked about an Italian or Mexican dinner the last time we were together at

Dr. Pendergast's funeral. Jerry and Juanita are offering the modern kitchen in their apartment where we can do some real fancy cooking."

"Oh boy, would I like that! Mrs. Martin, am I open this coming Saturday afternoon?"

Mrs. Martin leaves the room to check at the front desk where Roller's scheduling book is located.

"Believe me, Yolanda, if this schedule keeps up, either I get a couple of new physicians to help me out, or I really stay away from obstetrics."

"I hope not before I deliver my baby, Dr. Roller."

Mrs. Martin returns to the examining room.

"Good news, Dr. Roller, you are free this Saturday afternoon unless, of course, Mrs. Del Ocampo's baby decides to see this world earlier than predicted."

"Oh, tell that Mrs. Del Ocampo to keep her legs crossed until Sunday!" Juanita frowns as she speaks.

"Juanita!" Yolanda quiets down her younger sister.

CHAPTER 16

Yolanda's Apartment North Charleston

ON SATURDAY, JUANITA ARRANGES CUT flowers and places them in a vase as the three of them wait for Bill to arrive. The apartment is simply furnished, but neatly arranged for comfortable living. Jerry opens the door at first ring.

"Please come in, Dr. Roller. I'm Jerry, Juanita's husband. We sure are glad that you are able to join us for dinner this afternoon."

"I'm absolutely pleased to meet you, Jerry. Please just call me Bill. Hello, Juanita, Yolanda."

"Can I call you Bill too?" Juanita asks. "You know me better than Yolanda, I think!" Yolanda blushes.

"I'm not a doctor," Jerry interrupts, "but I can probably match Bill's interest in beers! I may not be able to match your experience in wine tasting, but Charleston has no less than a dozen breweries. We are the Palmetto State's craft beer capital!"

"Good to know that, Jerry. What do you do for the Navy? Yolanda told me that you are on active duty."

"I'm a warrant officer, a machinist at the Naval Support Activity just outside of the city."

"I was a reserve officer in the medical corps for a few years after my residency in San Diego. Yolanda must have told you about my taste for pilsner beer."

"Yes, she did. Here, please have a seat, and perhaps, I can get you something to drink?"

"Yes, I'd like some Charleston beer."

"Canned or bottled?"

"Either way as long as it's poured in a stein!"

"Sadly, a stein we don't have."

"Then bottled, please."

Juanita calls them to the table for dinner.

Before being seated, Bill clears his throat to get Juanita's attention.

"I have a little surprise for you, Juanita."

He takes a piece of paper with the hospital imprint on it out of his pocket. "Your pregnancy tests are positive. We really can call this a celebration dinner."

"Oh, thank you, Doctor, I mean, Bill." She glances at Jerry. "I… we hope it is another boy. We already have a room ready for him."

"Jerry, you take Juanita's glass, and let us have a toast for a healthy baby boy about seven months from now."

They toast and get ready to savor an Italian dinner. They all enjoy and leave not a bit to be eaten at another meal. It is good.

"I'm full and would very much like to use your restroom. Is it just down the hall?"

"Yes."

"I'll find it. Excuse me."

In the restroom, Bill Roller notices odd-looking tablets in a small pharmacy container that he is not familiar with. On it is listed Dr. Pendergast as the physician. He brings the container out to show to Juanita.

"I am not trying to be nosy, but while washing my hands, I noticed this bottle. Juanita, are you taking these?"

"Not yet. But I was meaning to ask you if I should take them. Dr. Pendergast told me that they are very special vitamin pills usually taken after the fourth month until the baby is born."

"I was concerned about that too, Bill," Yolanda adds. "I looked for them in the *Physicians' Desk Reference* book and couldn't find a match. I took one of them to our pharmacist, and he wasn't able to match it with any of the known medications at the pharmacy.

He looked concerned and asked me if he could send a sample to Zerxis Laboratories in Columbia for identification. I tried to reach you by phone at that time, but darn it, you were too busy, so I said go ahead. I have not heard back from him yet."

"Please let me know when you get the results, okay? May I take this container with me, Juanita?"

"Of course."

"I don't want you to take any until we are very sure of the medical makeup of these pills. Thank you for this delicious dinner, ladies. And I am so pleased to meet you, Jerry. Time to go."

"Likewise, Doctor. We hope we can have dinner with you again another time and soon."

Bill shakes hands, hugs the three, and leaves.

CHAPTER 17

Roller's Apartment

BILL FINDS SOME TIME TO relax in his apartment, puts his feet up, watches television, and samples one of Charleston's draft beers. His phone rings.

"Bill, I am very concerned," Yolanda starts. "I just received a call from a Dr. Siebertson from Zerxis Laboratories in Columbia. He has identified the capsules and wants to see me for a face-to-face discussion about it."

"That sounds serious."

"Do you think that maybe you can come with me?"

"I'll check my schedule. Perhaps, Mrs. Martin can arrange it so that I can."

"I'd be grateful if you could. I am mystified about a face-to-face."

CHAPTER 18

Zerxis Laboratories
Columbia, South Carolina

DR. SIEBERTSON, YOLANDA, AND DR. Roller are able to have the face-to-face meeting the following week on Friday morning. They meet at Zerxis Laboratories in Columbia. Although it is quite the trip, it is painfully important, and both Yolanda and Bill have to arrange for a day off to make the 110-mile drive.

The ride is, for the most part, very businesslike as each is deep into their own thoughts as to why this meeting has to be face-to-face. Obviously, something is very wrong with the medication or the delivery of said medication.

Little do they know the hornets' nest they are about to unleash.

Finding the laboratory is easy enough, and after a few wrong turns in the long hallways, the 9:00 AM meeting is to happen in Dr. Siebertson's cold laboratory-like office space.

Bill greets Dr. Siebertson and introduces Yolanda to him. "This is quite the setup you have here, Dr. Siebertson, all glass and metal—very modernistic."

"Thank you, Dr. Roller, and thank you both for coming. I do apologize for holding the *why*. It is a great, big *why* because I am very pro-life."

"Good God, Bill, I am glad you are with me. I may not be able to handle this alone."

Bill holds Yolanda's hand and asks Dr. Siebertson to continue.

"We are ready for it, Doctor. Please go ahead."

"First, I needed to chemically analyze the contents of this capsule before I could reach a final conclusion."

"It is not a vitamin pill, Doctor?" Yolanda asks.

"Definitely not. It is a compound synthesized and available only in some European countries."

"Which means that it is not approved by the FDA."

"Correct, Dr. Roller. The name is Zyatol. It is very similar to RU-486."

"The abortion pill?"

"Yes, Yolanda. Only much stronger."

Siebertson places a commercial poster showing the different parts of the placenta and fetus inside a human uterus on a board and points at different parts. He moves the pointer as he speaks.

"We all know that progesterone is needed by the woman to sustain pregnancy. Progesterone makes the placental cells work to keep the fetus alive.

"Zyatol not only blocks the action of progesterone on these trophoblastic cells, but it also makes the uterus contract to expel the developing fetus—like a double whammy."

"*Madre mia!*" Yolanda gasps.

"You mentioned that a physician administered this medication to a pregnant woman?"

"Yes, Doctor. My sister. Dr. Pendergast purposely aborted my sister's baby! But why?"

"That can't be right, Yolanda. I know that he even attended the pathological examination of the fetus, wondering why it happened. The official report only showed a normal twenty-week gestation of a male fetus.

"No, no. I just can't believe that Jules Pendergast could do such an awful thing. He was so pleasant to work with. There was only one time when he was visibly angry."

"When was that, Bill?"

"At about the time that Juanita lost her baby. Another patient of his went out of town without his permission, and he was so concerned that she might have problems."

"Did she, Bill?"

"I don't know. He never told me. The very next time I saw him was when I surprised him at the butcher shop. He was buying calf sweetbread for a meal Lorena was preparing for them."

"Well, that's about all I can tell you. I hope I've been helpful," Dr. Siebertson concludes their meeting.

"Thanks, Doctor. You've been a great help. You've left us with more questions at a time when we are looking more for great answers."

"Yes, Yolanda. That is why the great philosopher René Descartes said that medicine was more of an art than a science. You two have a pleasant drive back, ya hear? If ever you need me, I am always ready to assist you. I'd also like the answer."

CHAPTER 19

DCRF, Charleston

TWO UNIFORMED POLICEMEN HELP ELAINE get to the building through a throng of very angry protesters the following Thursday morning. Raising their fists and yelling, they are making certain that their voices are heard loud and clear. She finds Yolanda at the biochemistry laboratory, straightening her uniform as she monitors the emulsification process being performed by newly hired technologists.

"Thank God, you made it up safe, Elaine."

"Two cops helped me get through. They are really angry out there."

"It isn't much better in here either."

"So?"

"Somehow, a Dr. Frankle called Mr. Westerman and complained about something."

"This early in the morning?"

"Yeah."

"What could be that bad, I wonder?"

"Dr. Davidson is down in the animal lab right now, looking for Mr. Timmerman."

They stop talking as they see Westerman and Davidson coming out of the elevator and walking toward the radiation room. They look visibly upset. Yolanda notices Westerman's clenched fists. She and Elaine faintly hear him say, "The nerve. Seventy-five thousand for a set of four! As it is, sixty thousand is highway robbery already."

"Take it easy, Dave. I told you that we will hold off until the very last."

They walk briskly past them and quickly disappear inside the irradiation room. As fast as the door closes, it opens again. Davidson grabs their smocks with the radiation tags on and carries them both with him back into the room. The door closes.

"Hmm. Tell me, Elaine, what set of four can cost, say, sixty thousand dollars?"

"That's easy. Diamond earrings, necklace, brooch, diamond rings, perhaps? I once saw a diamond brooch that was priced almost a million dollars in a Neiman Marcus catalog."

"Then that couldn't be it."

"Tie this up together. Very angry mob outside, a call from another doctor, whoever he is, a talk with Mr. Timmerman downstairs, and two very upset bosses of a building being targeted..."

"Well, hello, Perry Mason Yolanda, you've got it. They are trying to settle the situation outside by bribery through that doctor who just called!"

"Yeah, but I still don't get it about the set of four."

"Ha, that's even easier. Four separate payments."

"Then they better get that going before somebody gets hurt or, worse, killed!"

CHAPTER 20

Pendergast Mansion Charleston

THE PENDERGAST HOME IS LOCATED in an older section of the city. It looks more like a renovated and modernized 1930s classic mansion of the South. Lorena greets Bill and Yolanda warmly.

"I apologize for not having you sooner, but I am still arranging some of Jules's unfinished bookwork." She points to a small desk with piles of paper in an adjacent room.

"We understand, Lorena. It must be very difficult for you."

"You know, Bill, when one dies unexpectedly, it leaves the survivor with so many unforeseen problems that need quick solutions."

"As far as the office and his practice are concerned, Lorena, please feel free to call me. I will be more than happy to help you."

"You have such a lovely home, Lorena." Yolanda walks around the formally decorated living room and admires paintings of the old South.

"Over the years, Yolanda, Jules and I were able to slowly collect things that we both admired and displayed. But let us all go into the dining room. I have dinner ready for us."

They settle down and enjoy a formal dinner served by two uniformed attendants. After dinner, Lorena gives them a tour of the house. As the two leave the home after formal, but pleasant good-byes, they continue to admire the surrounding old Charleston neighborhood before them.

Driving home, Bill notices how silent Yolanda has been.

"What's up?"

"When you were looking at Dr. Pendergast's display of old surgical instruments, I asked Lorena if she would share with me her sweetbread recipe. You said her husband was buying sweetbread for her from the butcher shop. I asked because I just couldn't find a way to fit it in during dinner."

"Did she?"

"She doesn't even know anything about sweetbreads—never heard the term nor knows how to fix it."

"I'm surely glad she served a roast beef meal. It was super delicious."

"You mean chateaubriand?"

"Oh, pardon my French, but do you get that every day up in Wisconsin?"

"You know that they have a yacht and summer beach home at Kiawah Island too?"

"I've always dreamed about that."

"Oh."

"Yes, a small beach home somewhere on Maui where—"

"Yolanda, Kiawah Island is right here in South Carolina! Don't mix the Pacific with the Atlantic."

"Okay, okay."

"I was just trying to figure it out in my head."

"What?"

"The opulence we just saw—"

"I'm all ears."

"Could not have come from Pendergast's earnings as a family physician no matter how busy he might have been."

"No?"

"I am now in charge of the office and have seen the figures of the last seven years. He earned an average of one hundred thirty thousand dollars a year.

That's simple."

"Simple?"

"Lorena is *vieux riche*, 'old money.' He married rich—smart guy! And no kids. Then I know what I'll do. It just dawned on me that you can't have kids…"

"Don't look at me like that, buddy boy, I'm not *vieux riche!*"

"Oh, I'm smart all right. By marrying you, I could be shopping at Neiman Marcus!"

They continue to enjoy the evening ride home through Charleston's business district. Bill points out a fancy well-lit department store.

"Maison Blanche! That must be just like Neiman Marcus."

"Oh, by the way, by doing that, you just jogged my memory."

"Shoot!"

"A few days ago we had demonstrators ready to tear the building apart outside. Cops needed to escort Elaine just to get her into the building. Then we heard Davidson and Westerman talking angrily about sixty thousand dollars for a set of four and someone wanting to up it to seventy-five thousand.

That was after some doctor called and talked to Timmerman up at our animal lab. Elaine and I overheard their conversation. We thought that they might be trying to pay the demonstrators some money in four installments through the doctor who called."

"That makes no sense at all. Paying people like those radicals off only means surrendering to them. They'll be asking for more and more later on. And who is their leader? It's simply more trouble."

Chapter 21

Military Academy Charleston

ON A BRIGHT SATURDAY MORNING, Dr. Archibald Frankle and Fowler Schmidt watch students practice parading exercises from the bleachers of Citadel Military Academy just outside the city.

"Dr. Frankle, you didn't come all the way here just to watch cadets go marching on a nice day like today with me. What is on your mind, sir?"

"Mr. Schmidt—"

"Please just call me Fowler."

"Fowler, the group of doctors I work with are very upset with what you did to Dr. Pendergast. Replacing him is almost next to impossible for us now."

"Doctor, you know your business, and I know mine."

"Getting rid of him the way you did was not what they had in mind."

"Well, as I just told you, sir, I got paid for a job that needed doing. I did it my own way. If you don't like the way I do things, please let me know. There are other people who may cost you less, and the outcome, not so drastic. You wanted him taken care of. In my field of expertise that means *dead*."

CHAPTER 22

Fort Sumter, South Carolina

TWO MEN WALK THE BATTLEMENT at Fort Sumter early the following Sunday morning. Jason Lee Janz is thirty-seven, thin, bearded, and looks as if he can pack a little more weight on just to fit into the clothes he is wearing.

Actually, he is an assistant professor in the history department of a university. He earns extra money by organizing protests for a big moneyman, John Kelp. He has a knack for inciting trouble.

With him is Manny Timmerman of the Davidson Cancer Research Foundation. They stop and look at the inscription on a historical plaque.

"This historical place is dear to my heart, Tim. The first shot of the Civil War was fired here. Do you know that? When the animal rights group elected me as group leader, I insisted that my swearing in be conducted here. I am very proud of it. And I am ready to do whatever I can to get our mandate carried out whatever it takes," Janz boasts and continues, "I feel like I am Fidel Castro or Paul Revere. It matters not—just special, I guess."

"You look more like a Count Dracula to me. You should try to get something good to eat every once in a while."

Posing like one of the characters in the movie *The Godfather*, Janz faces Timmerman.

"I've asked you to come this morning to give you an offer you can't refuse."

"And if I refuse?"

"I'll just offer you more money."

"Then how can I refuse?"

"Isn't that what I just told you?"

"What do you want me to do?"

"Now you're talking. And now listen carefully."

Janz turns his head around to ensure that nobody is within earshot of them.

"My group will make a timed little contraption that you should secretly place behind something in the animal laboratory. This thing should go *bang* and sort of rearrange things inside without killing any of the animals or hurting people. It should go off at a time when there isn't anybody in the building."

"Like nighttime."

"Precisely. We know that as a member of the staff there, you have the key to the building, and you are familiar with the locations in the interior."

"When do you want it to go *bang?*"

"I'll give you a call as soon as our little contraption is ready. I'll give you five hundred bucks now and another five hundred after we hear the *boom.*"

"Wow, how can I refuse that offer?"

"What did I tell you?"

"I've never done this sort of thing before, but what the heck! I'm good to go. I need the money. And no one will ever know it was me."

CHAPTER 23

Roller's Apartment

BILL RELAXES ON A COUCH in his apartment on a Friday evening two weeks later, watching the television news on the ongoing Balkan wars, when his phone rings. It is Yolanda on the line.

"Yes, Yolanda, I am watching TV too."

"Yeah, me too. If you are on the news, things are getting really hot inside that former Yugoslavian country, aren't they?"

"Yeah. But you must have thought of something else to sound so concerned."

"I am very concerned."

"Yes, Mrs. Freud. I can't stop thinking. My mind is a muddle of ideas trying to sort out the why and how and the money matters. I just can't relax."

Yolanda raises her voice, "Like Dr. Pendergast purposely aborting Juanita's baby, he and his wife living a life of questionable luxury, Pendergast lying about his wife wanting sweetbreads, Pendergast getting extraordinarily upset about one of his patients going out of town without letting him know, his sudden death, Davidson and Westerman missing a specimen at the biochemistry lab for the first time—"

"Stop right there. Something is, indeed, out of whack. Let me sleep on it overnight and call you tomorrow. I have something in mind and someone who might really be of help to us. She is chief librarian at the medical school here."

CHAPTER 24

Medical School Library Charleston

NOT TOO FAR FROM THE Davidson Cancer Research Center is the medical school. It is furnished with a modern and well-stocked research library, which is connected to a worldwide web of medical information. Chief Librarian Jeanette Dempsey cheerfully welcomes Bill and Yolanda. Bill introduces the two, who exchange appropriate pleasantries with each other. Dempsey is a stately black woman who has run the library for no less than twenty years.

Born and raised in New Orleans from a middle-class family, she literally mothers the medical students needing library assistance of any kind. She is very straightforward, most knowledgeable, and endowed with a wonderful sense of humor.

"Jeanne, we are pleased that you could find time this afternoon to help us," Bill starts.

"It's either I fit you in, Dr. Roller, or I spend the whole afternoon fighting with pesky medical students."

"Your building looks just awesome, Jeanne."

"Thanks, Yolanda. We have the latest in everything. If anything is written up or published anywhere in the world, we will find it for you. Some take time to get printed, others come out rather quickly and easily."

Dempsey takes them into a separate room away from the main part of the library. She has a wide-screen computer, keyboard, and printer all hooked up together. They find comfortable seating.

"Where shall we start, Dr. Roller? Give me your first index term."

"Let's start with *transforming factor gamma*."

"Okay." Dempsey keys in *transforming factor gamma* and says, "That's rather new to me."

They wait for the computer to respond. Nothing shows up on the screen, and the printer keeps quiet. They wait. Nothing happens.

"Something could be wrong with the computer or the Web, or there is really nothing about that particular tissue or chemical." Dempsey gives Roller a questioning glance.

"How about just *transforming factor*, Jeanne?"

"Here goes. I'm pretty sure we'll get something out of that."

Nothing happens.

"Let's try *cytokine*," Yolanda suggests.

"Good idea." Dempsey keys in *cytokine*.

Within almost a split second the printer starts whirring and printing pages upon pages as the screen comes to life with all kinds of information. Dempsey needs to manually stop the process.

"Well, there is obviously nothing wrong with your system, Jeanne."

"You are right about that, Dr. Roller, let's try something else."

"Let us now try another, Jeanne. Please enter *irradiated equine nervous tissue with transforming factor gamma*."

"Yes, that's what we use at the foundation," Yolanda agrees.

"That's what we should have been doing in the first place. Perhaps, we can find out the cytokine's true mechanism of action…"

"Or what Davidson claims the cytokine can do," Yolanda completes Jeanne's remarks.

"But first, let us see what we can find if we enter *natural equine nervous tissue with transforming factor gamma*," Dempsey suggests.

"You are the boss here."

"Okay, Dr. Roller, here goes."

There is no response.

"Next, then, we key in *irradiated equine nerve tissue with transforming factor gamma.*"

There is no response.

"Jeanne, will you please enter the whole enchilada, *irradiated equine nervous tissue, transforming factor gamma, and cancer treatment.*"

There is no response from the printer or screen.

"Holy crap! Oh, I'm sorry, Dr. Roller, but our system isn't able to be of help to you!"

"On the contrary, Jeanne, you have given us a lot of other things to worry about besides what's happening at the foundation. Thank you very much. If you don't mind, Yolanda and I will mentally digest what just took place here at the library and, perhaps, ask you again someday?"

"It will be a pleasure. Just call."

"Thank you!!"

On the ride back home Yolanda and Bill are both in deep thought. The almost half an hour of eerie silence is broken when Yolanda starts sobbing quietly.

"What's the matter, Yolanda?"

"Bill, we ransacked our brains on this matter, and we ended up flat on square one."

"No, we didn't."

"No?"

"Yep. As a matter of fact, we made a big leap."

"How?"

"I'm now convinced more than ever that your transforming factor gamma probably does not even exist. And that radiating horse nerve tissue does not produce anything at all that can cure cancer."

"What do we do next?"

"I tell you what. The medical staff just announced that a well-known visiting professor of endocrinology and physiology from the Midwest will be giving a talk next month at the Heinrich Educational Center of the hospital. His topic is on the endocrinological and physiological aspects of menstruation and pregnancy. Buffet dinner will be served.

All currently pregnant patients and their husbands are invited together with medical and paramedical staff. Two huge pharmaceutical companies are sponsoring this very special event."

"Are you going to attend?"

"Definitely, and I want you, Juanita, and Jerry to be there too. I think I still have one of the hospital flyers somewhere in my coat pocket." Roller searches his pockets. "It is very special because the hospital is celebrating its diamond jubilee. Ah, here's the flyer." He unfolds the flyer and shows it to Yolanda.

"Watch your driving. Give it to me, and I'll read it." Yolanda sees the picture of the speaker with his name under it. "Bill, Bill!"

"What, what!"

"I know this guy!" She shows Bill the lecturer's name: Bryan Joseph Lindbergh, MD, PhD.

"You know Dr. Lindbergh?"

"Yes, he is a professor at M-COW!"

"Wow! Does he know you?"

"Probably not. He was one of my professors when I was in college, but I know who might!"

"Who?"

"Elaine. If I remember correctly, Elaine told me that her father and Dr. Lindbergh were in the same medical school class!"

"Well, be sure that Elaine knows about this lecture, and please make sure she is with us at the conference."

CHAPTER 25

Physician's Office Maine

IT IS A REALLY FROSTY day, and the drive to the clinic is a bit unnerving in the new snow. Two women try to keep themselves warm while they talk about names for their forthcoming babies at a small medical office, which is blanketed with new fallen snow in Sleepy Creek, Maine. Their conversation is interrupted when a nurse calls one of them into the consultation room where the obstetrician is waiting.

"Mrs. Van Sallowry, the doctor is ready for you."

Sallowry enters the room. With a smile, the obstetrician offers her a seat and starts reviewing her records with her.

"Mrs. Van Sallowry, your ultrasound shows a healthy baby boy. Since this is your first pregnancy and you are now in your eighteenth week of gestation, we will need to be very careful.

"I have special vitamin pills for you to take twice a day. As much as possible please don't leave town, and let me know the minute you feel any discomfort or discharge at all, okay? These pills should sustain your pregnancy to term."

He hands her the prescription bottle of Zyatol capsules.

"Thank you, Doctor. Leaving town right now is beside the point, you know." She rolls her eyes and points to the frosted window as she leaves the room.

"I guess you are right. Do please keep warm!"

CHAPTER 26

Physician's Office Arizona

BLOOMING OCOTILLOS AND TALL DATE palm trees surround a medium-sized multispecialty clinic in Yucca Flats, Arizona. The obstetrics section is well ventilated and pleasantly decorated with desert plants and pictures of coyotes and scorpions. Two pregnant women argue about the true existence of the jackalope as they examine the stuffed animal display.

"Jennifer, just look at it, have you noticed this thing here before?"

"No, Rosie, but I've seen one of them somewhere in South Dakota."

"Live?"

"Stuffed like this one—on display at Wall Drugs, I believe."

A call from the nurse ends their conversation.

"Mrs. Donnelly, the doctor is ready for you."

Donnelly follows the nurse into the doctor's consultation room, where she is greeted warmly and seated.

"Mrs. Donnelly, your ultrasound shows a very healthy baby boy. Since this is your first pregnancy and you are now in your eighteenth week of gestation, we need to be very careful so that we can expect a smooth delivery. Please take this special vitamin complex, one capsule twice a day, before meals."

He hands her a prescription bottle of Zyatol capsules.

"Remember, please avoid leaving town over the next few weeks or even delivery time. And call me right away if you notice any pain, discomfort, discharge, or anything unusual at all."

"Yes, Doctor, I really don't intend to leave town. I can't wait to tell my husband, and by the way, is that really a real stuffed jackalope out in your foyer?"

"I really don't know." The doctor shakes his head and escorts her out of the room. "It was a gift."

CHAPTER 27

DCRF

THE AFTERNOON IS THE FOURTH consecutive day that is unusually quiet around the Davidson Cancer Research Foundation. For some reason it seems that the demonstrators have finally decided to leave the building alone. Patients in wheelchairs as well as on walkers or using decorative canes move in and out of the building freely. A limousine stops. A courier hurriedly enters the building.

Davros Westerman is on the fourth floor visiting with families of patients receiving their injections when his beeper starts beeping. He checks the message. It is a call from his secretary to let him know that a courier is waiting for him in his office.

He excuses himself and makes his way to the elevator and down to his office as quickly as possible to meet the courier.

The courier hands Westerman the box that is labeled, "Packed in Dry Ice." "Sir, this is from Dr. Frankle's office."

"Okay, let's see." Westerman nods as he diligently opens the box, lifts four small hard plastic containers, each with whitish tissues inside. He gives the courier an approving nod and discards the box into a large receptacle nearby labeled "Hazardous Material." Then he carefully places them into a plastic box and stashes it inside a dumbwaiter on the wall.

He pushes a lighted green button next to the dumbwaiter. He walks into a closet behind his desk and, after a few minutes, returns carrying a briefcase. He opens the briefcase and shows the courier stacks of one-hundred-dollar bills totaling sixty thousand dollars.

"Here is the money, please count it if you wish."

"Yes, sir. Dr. Frankle instructed me to make sure of the amount." Finding the correct amount, he thanks Davros Westerman.

"Please give my regards to Dr. Frankle, will you?"

"Yes, sir." The courier leaves with the briefcase.

Right after the courier leaves, Westerman picks up the phone and dials a number.

Waiting in the irradiation room, Davidson answers the phone immediately.

"Yes, Dave. I have them. I'll put them in the freezer." Davidson unlocks the freezer.

He carefully labels the box with Dr. Frankle's name and places it in alphabetical order with other physicians' names on them, which are already in the freezer.

On top of a nearby desk is a computer. He turns the computer on and checks a box on a spreadsheet with Dr. Archibald Frankle's name, address, and phone numbers on it. Other physicians' names and information are listed on the same spreadsheet.

He pushes the Copy button and removes a floppy disk. He places the floppy disk in his coat pocket and leaves the room. Westerman meets him as he leaves and ushers him back into the irradiation room with him.

"Problems, Dave?"

"Maybe not, but are you certain that Ms. Ybarra is still unaware of what we're doing here?"

"She's a med-technologist and one of the best, Dave. Aside from the obvious excitement we all notice in her when Dr. Roller is visiting, she does nothing, but concentrate on the job at hand."

"Okay, it's just that I, at one time, noticed her looking at my radiation counter when I accidentally came into this room without it."

"Well, then let's just be careful and not think about that anymore, okay? By the way, Dave, do we have enough money in the safe to pay the courier from Arizona should he be here within the next few days?"

"Yes, we do. We have almost a million in one-hundred-dollar bills in our safe."

"That ought to be enough. Yes, and the cash just keeps on coming. You know that we each have around fifty million dollars in Swiss bank accounts. I am even thinking of investing in a hotel or inn to house relatives of patients' families who oftentimes find difficulty in getting accommodations locally."

"Hey, that's not a bad idea. We will be our own Ronald McDonald House."

"Remember that fellow Mr. Eastwood from Bradford and Associates?"

"You've got to be kidding, I can't even remember what I had for breakfast yesterday or if I even had breakfast."

"Well, I'll try to get hold of him within the next few days and see what he can come up with."

"There should be room on either side of the building for another construction. Let us see what he thinks."

CHAPTER 28

St. Bonaventure Hospital

THE HEINRICH EDUCATIONAL CENTER IS in a separate, smaller building adjacent to St. Bonaventure Hospital. In addition to the large, auditorium-style classroom, there are several smaller rooms dedicated to small groups for in-service training, CPR, advanced cardiac life support (ACLS), and advanced trauma (ATLS) life support.

There are also mannequins and a small operating suite for animals, where laparoscopic surgery is constantly being updated by physicians and surgeons.

Next to the large lecture room is a smaller room where pharmaceuticals, books, and surgical instruments are displayed by representatives who are busily demonstrating their products to potential buyers. Doctors, staffers, and spouses push to get to the front of the gathering crowds, pushing and shoving for some very fancy handouts not related to medicine at all. One can come away with small gifts priced in the hundreds of dollars.

Hospital staff, physicians, patients, families, and guests sit comfortably and wait for the lecture to start.

Soon enough, the hospital director introduces Dr. Bryan Joseph Lindbergh, the guest lecturer, who wastes no time in getting into the subject matter at hand.

"Members of the hospital staff, ladies, and gentlemen, thank you for getting me out of the cold Midwestern weather and giving me a very warm welcome in Charleston. I see that many of us here are going to have babies pretty soon. If you don't mind, I'd like to have you rise, ladies, so that we can applaud you."

Pregnant women rise from their seats to be recognized. They acknowledge the applause from Lindbergh and the rest of the attendees.

Lindbergh continues, "This is the primary reason why I've been invited to speak to you on the physiology of pregnancy, menstruation, and the role the brain plays. Some people consider pregnancy as a condition or some kind of illness. No. It is a normal process of life itself. Without pregnancy, none of us would be here. Getting pregnant is usually no problem at all. It is oftentimes fun. Maintaining the pregnancy until birth, however, can be tricky sometimes."

Lindbergh shows a slide of a sagittal section of the human brain.

"As with all functions of the human body, direction comes from our brain. As far as development of the fetus goes, the hypothalamus"—he points at the structure located at the base of the brain—"is the commander in chief." He replaces the slide with a picture of a fetal brain and points at the fetal hypothalamus.

He continues, "The baby's tiny hypothalamus, which is located at the base of the brain, develops as early as the eighth week of gestation. It gets to the size of a small marble by the twentieth week and to the size of a walnut in adults. All the time it acts as a message center and commander.

It receives messages from all parts of the body and transforms them into command messages to the pituitary gland, which, in turn, transmits them to different organs in the body such as the thyroid gland et cetera."

"He really gets into details. I hope our nonmedical guests can understand him," Roller wonders.

Lindbergh continues, "As a young girl matures, the hypothalamus sends messages via the pituitary gland to start the process of menstruation."

He now shows a slide of the uterus. "Menstruation results from a decrease in progesterone level. In pregnancy, there is no such decrease. Progesterone sustains the cells that nourish the growing baby. Therefore, anything that blocks this process will cause a miscarriage."

Lindbergh continues on to finish his talk. Then the hospital director ushers him to the dining area where a sumptuous buffet is waiting.

"Let's go catch him." Elaine pulls Yolanda with her as Roller and the rest of their small group follow. They catch him right after he has filled his plate with food.

"Dr. Lindbergh, my name is Elaine Franche, you might remember Dr. Marshall Franche? I am his daughter."

"From Elm Grove? Yes! Sweet little Elaine, didn't you play with my boys when you kids were little?"

"Yes, sir. I had a lot of fun with them."

"I see your dad quite frequently at medical society meetings. What are you doing here in Charleston?"

"I am a medical technologist at the Davidson Cancer Research Foundation. I'd like you to meet my friends here." She introduces Roller, Ybarra, Juanita, and Jerry to Lindbergh. "Yolanda and Juanita are from Waukesha, you know."

"Oh my gosh, now I feel at home right here in Dixie."

"Your talk was just great, Dr. Lindbergh," Roller states.

"You don't think it was too technical?"

"No, sir," Ybarra answers.

"Did you say that you girls work at Davidson's?"

"Yes, sir. Yolanda is my boss," Elaine answers.

"We've been quite successful with our transforming factor gamma treatment for terminal cancer," Yolanda boasts.

"With what?"

"Transforming factor gamma, Dr. Lindbergh. We extract it from irradiated equine nerve tissue."

"Wait a minute, am I hearing this wrong, or are we that close to Disney World?"

"That's what I was afraid you'd say, Doctor," Roller agrees, shaking his head.

"And you, Bill, you are a doctor. Do you buy into this, this transforming factor gamma?"

"You can't fight success, sir. Nobody believed Dr. Semmelweiss when he tried to tell his colleagues that deadly bugs do exist and that they can be washed off quite easily."

"Or when Galileo told the church that the earth moves around the sun. I think he was even jailed for that."

Lindbergh looks for a place to sit as Bill, Yolanda, Elaine, Jerry, and Juanita pick up their plates and go to get some food.

For quite a few days, constant worrying has been hiding Yolanda's lovely Hispanic facial features, which she enhances with a small degree of makeup. She needs a bit of sympathy from Bill and calls him in the morning just before she heads for work.

"Bill, what did you think of Dr. Lindbergh's lecture? I'm wondering because I haven't heard from you."

"As far as the way the lecture went, it was really to the point. It took me back to medical school days when we dissected brains and studied the hypothalamus under a microscope. But I felt silly at what he said to me."

"Like?"

"Did I not question transforming factor gamma, being the physician whom I claim to be? I felt so embarrassed."

"That is bugging me too."

"I tell you what. Let's get back to that research library and dig some more. There's got to be more to it than what that superintelligent Lindbergh knows."

CHAPTER 29

Medical School Library

IT IS ALREADY PAST THE regular library hours, and just a few students are around looking for printed journals, but just the same, Jeanne Dempsey cheerfully welcomes Bill and Yolanda back to her research screen and printer.

"I went ahead and primed the computer right when you called, Dr. Roller. It is working perfectly."

"Thanks, Jeanne."

"Do you have a new magic combination of items you and Yolanda want researched this time?"

"You bet."

"Then let's get going."

"Please start with *sixteen—to twenty-week gestation, male fetus, first pregnancy,* and *brain.*"

"No kidding?"

"None."

The printer spits pages after pages of scientific articles.

"There is nothing wrong with your system, Jeanne."

"I thought I just told you that, Yolanda."

"Let us narrow it down a bit, okay?

"Right on, Dr. Roller."

"Bill, perhaps, we should include the hypothalamus. Dr. Lindbergh talked about that a lot."

"Who is Dr. Lindbergh, Yolanda? Is he a son or something of the famous Charles Lindbergh?"

"I don't know. He is from Wisconsin."

"How, what—"

"Jeanne," Roller interrupts, "he was at the Heinrich Educational Pavilion of the hospital and gave a talk on pregnancy and the hypothalamus recently."

"Oh, okay. Let us key in *hypothalamus, male fetus, first pregnancy, sixteen—to twenty-week gestation.* Is this what you want, Dr. Roller?"

"Why not, since we are all playing?"

Seven European and one American abstracts come out of the printer. They also appear on the screen. They all show a cytokine called prototensin.

"Prototensin? That is new to me. Jeanne, are there papers on what this prototensin does or can do?"

"Let us see."

The printer prints a single page of paper on prototensin. Roller scans the articles.

"Here is one on prototensin and mice melanoma. Written by a Jean Marie Guthrie, MD, PhD."

"Where in the world is this Dr. Guthrie from, Jeanne?"

"Let us find out."

Within a few seconds Dr. Guthrie's data shows up on the screen.

"There she is, Dr. Roller. University of California in San Francisco."

"Oh, Bill, take me there," Yolanda pleads. "I want to see San Francisco. That is where Tony Bennett left his heart, you know."

With a bit of a tease, Dempsey agrees. "Yes, Dr. Roller, take Yolanda there. You might find something else besides Tony Bennett's lost heart."

CHAPTER 30

Research Laboratory, UCSF

THE UNIVERSITY MEDICAL COMPLEX LOOKS impressive. It overlooks the Pacific Ocean when on a clear day one can see cruise ships and ordinary sailing vessels sail over the peaceful waves. Today, it is cloudy. And a mist has just drifted in from the ocean, impairing visibility.

Dr. Guthrie's office is located on the eighth floor of the main building. Bill and Yolanda have no trouble finding the elevator, which takes them where they need to be. A well-groomed, neatly dressed, aristocratic tall, bespectacled, 50-ish-looking lady greets them as they enter the clean, neatly furnished laboratory.

"Good morning. I am Jean Marie Guthrie. I've been waiting for you. I was, indeed, very excited to get your call a couple of days ago."

"Good morning, Doctor. I am Bill Roller, and this is my friend, medical technologist Yolanda Ybarra."

"I am certainly very pleased to meet you. Did you have any trouble coming here from the East Coast?"

"The flight from Chicago was a little bumpy at times, Doctor," Yolanda answers.

"Dr. Guthrie—"

"Please call me Jean, Dr. Roller."

"Then call me Bill. It's just that…"

"I am really younger than I look."

Everybody smiles at one another and relaxes.

"Bill, Yolanda, I am really extremely excited to know that you, young and bright scientists, have expressed a genuine interest in my work on prototensin. I must admit that it has slowed down a bit. At least now I can converse with somebody in this country about my progress instead of calling Germany all the time."

"Germany?"

"Yes, Bill, you know that the cytokine was first isolated in Bavaria."

"Is that where Heidelberg University is?" Yolanda asks Dr. Guthrie.

"Yes, Yolanda."

"Problems, Yolanda?"

"I don't know, Bill. But Dr. Davidson received his PhD from Heidelberg University."

"It's most likely just a coincidence," Guthrie assures Yolanda. "Heidelberg is a fabulous institution for both science and art."

"Yes, Jean. As a kid, my parents took me to see that movie *The Student Prince*. I was a little bored, but my parents enjoyed it."

"That's beside the point, Bill. How far along are you guys on your prototensin work?"

Bill and Yolanda look at each other.

"As a matter of fact, Doctor, we don't even know what it is," Bill answers sheepishly.

"What?" Guthrie explodes like a Molotov cocktail.

For the first time she doesn't look like the distinguished university professor that she is.

"Beg your pardon, ma'am, but…but really, Yolanda and I came here to learn from you."

"All the way from the East Coast."

"Really, ma'am, all the way from the East Coast," Yolanda agrees.

"Then I might have to start from the beginning."

"I wish you would. It's why we are here."

"Firstly, what, in heaven's name, do you know about prototensin?"

"Yolanda and I were at the medical library, searching for the most recent, still unproven, but could potentially be very effective treatment for cancer."

"Bill, were you at the last ASCO convention in Chicago? I had an exhibit and gave a talk there."

"Ass who?"

"ASCO, meaning American Society of Clinical Oncology."

"No. I… I…was not at that meeting."

"Ma'am, Bill is a family practitioner, not an oncologist."

"Oh dear, we really do have to start from the baseline. And I'm happy to do that. I rarely get someone so intensely interested in my first love, prototensin."

Guthrie leads the two into a room where there is a huge, black-and-white picture of a mammalian cell.

"As you know, this cell, whether it is a lymphocyte or a macrophage, if irritated by a toxin or any kind of irritant, produces an enzymelike substance, like cytokine." Like an elementary school-teacher, she taps at the picture with a wooden pointer stick in rapid succession.

"One of the better-known cytokines is cachectin, which can produce shock."

"Like toxic shock syndrome?"

"Yes, Bill."

"During the early gestation of the mammalian embryo, a cyto-kine, prototensin, is produced by the developing stem cells. What excites or stimulates the stem cells to do that has been investigated by scientists all over the world without finding an adequate answer.

It is most likely from an antigenetic fetal overexpression to a genetically inspired maternal hybridization that occurs only at initial gestation."

"Wow, can you say that in English?" Bill asks.

"Or Spanish!" Yolanda asks.

Guthrie pauses and moves to another part of the room where there is a large diagrammatic illustration of the fetal brain.

"You are both familiar with this fetal hypothalamus." She taps her pointer on the hypothalamus.

"Of course."

"For some unknown reason the fetal hypothalamus extracts this circulating prototensin and concentrates it."

"All mammalian fetal hypothalami, including human?"

"Yes, Bill."

"First pregnancy, male fetus, during, say, the sixteenth or eighteenth week of gestation?"

"Exactly. Only first pregnancies."

"Good God!" Yolanda exclaims.

"And what can this prototensin do?"

"Some believe that prototensin protects the fetus from developing intrauterine carcinomas. But that is debatable."

"Let me show you what it can do in laboratory animals." Guthrie takes them to a glass-enclosed section of the laboratory where they all don hazmat protective outfits.

"We have to wear this to protect the laboratory animals from outside contamination, Yolanda."

"We understand."

As soon as they get inside and close the door, Guthrie picks up a petri dish from a table.

"This is a culture where you can see dark spots, which are multiple and healthy growths of mice melanomas. You can see how abundant the growths are."

They see multiple small, dark-blue, and dark-brown spots on a field of teal-colored culture medium.

"Wow, I've never seen that at med tech school."

"Don't feel bad, Yolanda, I never saw that in medical school either."

"And now I have three vials here—a vial containing five-fluorouracil, a known anticancer drug, adriamycin, an anticancer antibiotic, and an emulsion of prototensin-rich fetal hypothalami."

She opens a small laboratory incubator and picks up three separate petri dishes. She shows them one at a time.

"This first dish of mice melanoma is untreated, and you can see the growths very similar to the one I showed you before. This next one is mice melanoma plus five-fluorouracil. You see how abundant the growths are. This next one is mice melanoma with adriamycin. There might be a little decrease in the number of cultures, but basically unaffected. This last one is mice melanoma with prototensin. As you can see, there is absolutely no growth."

All they see is teal-colored medium in the dish with no spots at all.

"Good heavens, Yolanda. Can you see that? Prototensin is one hundred percent effective!"

"Yes, Bill. I have cultures of guinea pig adenocarcinomas and squamous cell carcinomas showing the same effective results with prototensin."

"How, in heaven's name, does it work, Dr. Guthrie?"

"I thought you'd never ask. Let me show you. It is no secret at all. Oncologists all over the world know this."

"Something they never taught me in family-practice school."

They walk out of the special room into a more comfortable room, removing their hazmat outfits as they go. Here Dr. Guthrie replaces her picture of the cell with a circular representation of the mammalian cell cycle.

She starts, "Picture this as the face of a clock. The first growth period covers the space between the eleven and two o'clock positions. The two o'clock to the seven o'clock position is covered by the DNA synthesis phase or what we commonly know as the S phase."

"Is that where the cell uses all available energy and enzymes to grow?"

"Yes, Yolanda, and then prepare themselves to multiply."

"Here lies the difference between the cancer cell and the normal cell," Guthrie continues.

"The normal cell has a very slow, but strong S phase. The cancer cell has a very rapid, but weak or easily disrupted S phase. The more aggressive or undifferentiated the cancer cell, the weaker is its S phase."

"Oh god, that makes sense, Bill."

"What makes sense, Yolanda?"

"Uh, Dr. Guthrie, we treat only patients with undifferentiated carcinomas at our treatment center."

"That's good. Let me continue."

"Please, Doctor."

"Now, the segment between the seven and eleven o'clock position is covered by the second growth phase—the doubling phase, the mitotic stage, where the cell itself doubles its size. In very aggressive cancer cells this can be as brief as thirty minutes. However, the cell's capacity to divide depends on its integrity during the S phase. If you deprive the cell of the necessary enzymes it needs during the S phase, it cannot divide. It just dies. This is true in normal as well as cancer cells."

"So what happens to the normal cells in the body?"

"As I mentioned before, normal cells have very strong S phases."

"Is this where prototensin works?"

"Exactly, Bill. Prototensin is the only cytokine we have in the whole world, so far, which will selectively deprive cells of necessary enzymes they need to carry on their mitotic process. The weaker the S phase, the stronger prototensin works."

"Where do you get your prototensin?"

"From the minced hypothalami of fetal mice, Bill."

"From minced hypothalami of fetal mice?"

"Yes, Yolanda. May I show you how we obtain them?"

"Oh, please."

"Then follow me."

Guthrie leads them to another section of the laboratory where they need to wear just caps, masks, and surgical gowns over their clothes. Hazmat booties are not required. She takes them to a dissecting microscope connected to multiple eyepieces for at least half a dozen viewers. Under the microscope is a surgically opened head of a fetal mouse.

"We carefully dissect out the hypothalamus of the fetal mouse from its brain and emulsify it in Surgigel."

"Is that common gelatin, Dr. Guthrie?"

"Oh no, this is especially manufactured in France for surgical use only."

"Then we spin it in the high-speed centrifuge for five hours."

"Bill, this is eerie. We spin a very similar emulsion at the foundation for exactly the same time."

Guthrie continues, "We pipette out the precipitate, which is the prototensin, and reconstitute it with sixty micro cubic millimeters of the same Surgigel, put it in a Pyrex vial, and store it in the freezer. We repeat the process three times to get four vials of prototensin."

"You sacrifice four gestational mice to get their fetal hypothalami?"

"Not necessarily, Bill. These mice usually have multiple fetuses in their uteri. We only select the males."

"And at first pregnancies?"

"Yes, Yolanda."

"At what stage in their gestations do you sacrifice these animals?"

"At about the sixteenth day of mice gestation. We check them all by ultrasound."

Yolanda starts counting something with her fingers. "Dr. Guthrie, will that equate to about sixteenth week in human gestation?"

Guthrie smiles. "If you were a mouse, yes, Yolanda. Roughly."

They leave the room, removing their caps, gowns, and masks as they go to settle down on comfortable couches in an adjacent lounge.

"Well, Bill, Yolanda, what do you think of our research facility here?"

"You have educated us so much more and at warp speed and more than what we can truly comprehend, Jean."

"If you have suggestions, Bill, please tell me. We can always improve on what we have here already."

Bill looks at Yolanda and takes a deep breath before he speaks.

"Jean, I mean, Dr. Guthrie, is there reason to believe that, perhaps, prototensin therapy is already going on in this country?"

"Impossible! Prototensin has not been synthesized anywhere in the world yet! I've spent a lot of my time trying to clone the cytokine, and even that failed."

"Dr. Guthrie," with tears welling in Yolanda's eyes, she asks.

"Yes, Yolanda?"

"You don't need to synthesize the cytokine if you can get it from the mutilated brains of helpless unborn children!" Yolanda weeps loud and openly as she speaks.

"Good God, what are you talking about?"

"Jean."

"Yes, Bill?"

"From what you told us and what Yolanda and I have pieced together, it may be that the Davidson Cancer Research Foundation is already using prototensin, acquired from human fetal hypothalami, to treat their cancer patients."

"That just cannot be true, and I'll tell you why. I have two good reasons. One, they need four to five fetal hypothalami to treat every one of their patients, and two, they are reporting only a handful of complete recoveries from the thousands of patients they see each year. You've seen how effective prototensin is. If they were truly using prototensin, their reporting would near one hundred percent cures!"

"Dr. Guthrie, we report only thirty to forty-five percent cure rate, which is nothing short of phenomenal at that. Could it be that not all aggressive and undifferentiated cancer cells have weak S phases?"

"Come to think of it, Yolanda, yes. A human cancer cell may behave much differently from our in vitro mammalian cells here. Who knows?"

"Jean, can you extract prototensin from irradiated equine nerve tissues?"

"No, Bill. Radiation deactivates prototensin. It is very radio-sensitive. And prototensin is species specific. We have never been successful in treating guinea pig cancer by using mice prototensin."

"Dr. Guthrie, you really don't know how much you have helped us. More than ever, Yolanda and I are determined to find out what is truly going on at the Davidson Cancer Research Foundation. Thank you ever so much!"

"I am always here to help you. My interest is piqued for moral and medical reasons. Please call me again anytime. You two, please enjoy the rest of your time in San Francisco, and have a pleasant, safe flight home."

CHAPTER 31

Magnolia Park

BILL SELECTS AN ORNATE WROUGHT-IRON park bench shaded from the late afternoon sun. A magnificent magnolia tree stands behind him. He watches the mini horses romp around inside a fenced-in quadrangle and savors the pleasant scent of the abundant yellow jasmine, which are in bloom just behind him.

He hears footsteps coming from behind him and turns around.

"Woman, you are late!"

"Bill, so sorry, we had an emergency at the foundation, and I could not leave."

"Now, Yolanda, that's new. An emergency where you treat terminally ill patients? Did he die before you had the chance to treat him?"

"In a way, yes. He was only forty-six years old from Houston, Texas. He had metastatic pancreatic cancer and went into anaphylactic shock when we gave him the test dose of—now I know exactly what it is—Surgigel."

"Did you ever see that happen before?"

"No, the worst that I've seen before was last year—a thirty-five-year-old woman with advanced breast cancer who developed hives after a test dose. That was all. Well, we called for the ambulance when this guy started having difficulty of breathing. Thank God for paramedics. They came right away, intubated him, got a good IV running, and took him to St. Bonaventure Hospital."

"At least you knew exactly what to do with the patient."

"Have you been waiting long, Bill?"

"Oh, about half an hour. I was enjoying watching those mini horses cavort like crazy inside that fence."

Bill points to the enclosure.

"Bill, I know what you want to talk about to me this afternoon, and I know it's not about mini horses."

Yolanda sits down next to Bill.

"What are we going to do, Yolanda?"

"Okay, Bill. First let us talk about the evidence we have."

"Evidence? We have none."

"But from what we know already, we can forget about transforming factor gamma, which does not exist at all, and we know that for certain now."

"Yolanda, could they be irradiating something else inside that room, not equine nerve tissue as they claim?"

"Yeah, and using ultraminimal doses not enough to be picked up by their radiation dosimeters? Hmm. But it is true that Pendergast purposely aborted my sister's first baby, which was a boy, at exactly the same gestational time that human prototensin should be abundant in his hypothalamus. That alone is murder!"

"And I still remember what Adriane Eastwood said about miscarrying their first baby, another male, after taking those special vitamin pills, which we now know as Zyatol, Yolanda."

"Figure this out, Bill. Say we have eight thousand or ten thousand cures a year as we have so many times bragged about it. At four hypothalami each, we are sacrificing thirty-two thousand to forty thousand poor, defenseless male babies to cure terminal cancer patients, some of whom are too old and are going to die soon anyway."

"You are not God, Yolanda. Some of those kids may have grown up to be Hitlers and Al Capones..."

"Or Einsteins and Picassos, Bill."

They walk around the park and select another ornate wrought-iron bench to sit on. This one overlooks a stream of gently flowing water.

"Yolanda, I didn't ask you to meet me here just to talk about prototensin and transforming factor gamma. There is something else."

"What is it, Bill?"

"I found something else in San Francisco, and it is not Tony Bennett's lost heart."

Inching closer to Yolanda and placing his arm around her shoulders, entangling his hand in her beautiful curls, he turns her toward him and takes a small box from his jacket pocket with his free hand and says, "I found mine, and I give it all to you."

With Bill handing the small box to Yolanda, she takes a deep breath and, with shaking hands, clasps it.

"Open it, sweetheart. I can hardly wait, and I need your answer."

Gasping, she peers at a one-carat red ruby ring offset by two perfect diamonds set in platinum.

"Yolanda, I love you. I have loved you since the first time we met. Will you marry me?"

"Oh, Bill, yes, oh yes!"

Tears welling up in her eyes, she has him place the ring on her finger and, for a moment, sits still. She turns toward him and grabs his lapels, pulls him toward her, and kisses him with such intense feeling.

"Yes!"

"Really, yes?"

Lost somewhere between time and space the two just hold on to each other.

"Oh, Bill, I just have to show off my beautiful ring to Juanita and Jerry. Let's go there now."

"Not before we get something to eat. I can't tell you how hungry this makes a fellow."

"The Crab Shack is not far from here."

"Oh no, Yolanda, I am thinking of a nice large, juicy steak."

"Then there's got to be a steak house near here."

Hurrying to get out of the park, the two never notice a man walking about, admiring lovely roses, and savoring their perfume as he walks. Manny Timmerman soon finds a comfortable shaded park bench to sit on.

Minutes later, sitting on the bench, he finds himself deep in thought, not even noticing the squirrel that he is looking at, playing on the ground just inches away from his feet.

Both he and the squirrel are surprised when Jason Janz suddenly speaks from behind the bench.

"Why don't you give that poor thing something to eat? He must really be hungry. You didn't even notice me come from behind you."

Stunned, Timmerman gets up and turns around, recognizing Jason.

"Jason, don't scare me like that! You scared the hell out of me."

"You look like the police caught you red-handed setting up an explosive device on a plane ready to take off."

"Hey, this is no joke, Jason. I was in deep thought trying to figure out the best place for me to place that…that contraption of yours without killing any animals when it goes off. I love those animals, you know. I've been taking care of them for a long time."

"Hey, we are all animal lovers. The purpose is to destroy as much of their equipment as possible without killing the animals. You are our best choice to do that."

"I can see that. We have a storage closet that is set aside for brooms, cans, waste, and things. That might be the best place. It is far enough away from the animal cages and close enough to dissecting equipment, microscope, and other surgical instruments. Are you sure that that…that thing that you have will be strong enough to blow that closet door away?"

"The people who prepared this know their business. Just set the timer for nighttime when nobody should be in the building. We do not intend to kill people either."

The two sit on the bench next to each other.

"Tim, or Manny—"

"Just call me Tim. People at work call me Manny."

They are almost just whispering although they are isolated and the park is almost empty of visitors. Jason sits closer to Timmerman.

"In this suitcase, I have the contraption and five hundred dollars in cash. They are in the same plastic container. Do not—and I repeat—do not leave the money with the contraption when you set the timer."

"If you say one more insulting joke, you, you numbskull, I will set that damn bomb right now and blow us both to kingdom come!" Timmerman answers angrily.

"I truly beg your pardon. I didn't realize that you have absolutely no sense of humor at all."

"Listen! What you want me to do is something that I've never dreamed I'd do had I not needed the money so much."

"Okay, I do apologize again. I am very sorry. I never thought my group of people would ask me to do something this drastic either. After the *boom*, we will meet again the day after, whenever that day will be, in this very same area and time of day. I will give you the rest of the money, five hundred dollars, okay? And I am not joking."

"Okay. When do you want me to set this up?"

"Two weeks from now, on a Friday, there will be a big, but unusually very peaceful demonstration at your foundation with the people just singing, praying, and walking around. That will be your clue. The *boom* should take place that very same night."

"Okay." Timmerman takes the suitcase from Janz and walks away. After a short while, Jason leaves.

Driving out of the park, Bill spots a restaurant that features steaks from Texas, using mouthwatering large photographs. He points at one of the pictures.

"Sweetheart, that's my kind of meal!"

"Then, darling, let's go for it. You certainly deserve it."

"Do I ever!"

"And what do you mean by that?"

"I came to the East Coast armed with medical knowledge I believed would be difficult for any physician to repudiate."

"And?"

"Twice I've been badly humiliated."

"By whom...when?"

"Full of confidence, I agreed with you when we told Dr. Lindbergh that we use transforming factor gamma to cure cancer patients at the foundation."

"And his answer was…"

"Yes, I know. He said, 'Am I hearing this wrong, or are we that close to Disney World here?' I felt like a complete medical idiot!"

"But you had an unbelievable comeback, about some Dr. Semmelweiss, that he understood."

"That was the first one."

"Go on."

"Then we go to San Francisco."

"And?"

"Dr. Guthrie asked me, was I at that ASCO convention in Chicago? I asked, 'Ass-who?'"

Yolanda laughs, "Ass-who? That was really, really, really great."

"What do you mean?"

"Before you raised your hand, I was going to ask her why, in heaven's name, there should be an ascot convention, meaning the cravat that English men wear, like in the movie *My Fair Lady*."

"Then you excused my ignorance by telling her that I was just a family practitioner."

"That was really amusing."

"Amusing? My foot! She then said she would really need to start from the beginning."

Yolanda starts laughing.

"What's so amusing, sweetheart?"

"Remember her telling us about how weak the cancer cell's S phase is compared to normal cells? We tell that to all new hires at the foundation during their orientation. I felt like saying, 'Elementary, my dear Watson.'"

"I'm glad you did not. You could've had quite a shiner."

"Then, Bill Roller, I've seen you when you were at your best and when you felt humiliated. I still love you, and now I know that I am really qualified to be your wife."

"Yolanda, we are, indeed, ready to tackle whatever destiny God has laid down for us, for better or for worse. I love you. Let's get something to eat. I'm still starved."

He parks the car, and they head to the restaurant as she says, "I had better learn to really cook just to keep up with your appetite."

As they enter the restaurant, a blonde waitress, neatly dressed in Western attire, wearing white boots, greets them and ushers them readily into a very informal, but comfortable, and rather secluded booth for two. She notices Yolanda's ring.

"Wow, that's a beautiful ring!"

"We are celebrating our engagement," Bill answers.

"Oh dear, congratulations! We have a special dessert for you this evening, and it is on the house."

"What a deal. Thank you." The waitress hands them the menu and leaves.

Yolanda scans the menu as Bill looks at the old photographs of *Buffalo Bill's Wild West* show hanging on the wall, each one more intriguing than the last.

"Bill, do you know what you want from the menu?"

"Yes, that thing." He points at a big ad showing a T-bone steak. "Rare."

In almost no time at all, the waitress is back armed with a pen and a small pad of paper.

"First, let me get your drink order, and you can tell me what you two would like."

Bill points at the ad. "That T-bone, rare, with all the trimmings, and a mug of dark local beer."

"You got it, sir, and for you, ma'am?"

Yolanda points at the menu. "This steak Diane, medium rare, double-baked potato, and a glass of diet Coke with ice."

"Coming right up, ma'am." With a polite bow the waitress smiles and leaves.

Bill looks at the ring and Yolanda's face back and forth like a Wimbledon tennis fan.

"Is there anything wrong, sweetheart?"

"No. I'm just trying to figure out when I can meet your parents and when you can meet mine."

"You can meet mine right around October 6. That's my birthday. I was born on October 6, 1971."

"That's not too far away."

"I can also take you to Holy Hill. The maple trees there should be in peak coloration."

"And that makes this hill holy? What other crazy things do you have up there in Wisconsin, a red river or something?"

"No, but we have a Black Earth. Listen, wise guy. Holy Hill is a Carmelite shrine on top of a hill in Wisconsin. It was founded in 1862."

"Oh, okay. We should go to San Diego around May 11, okay? I was born on May 11, 1967."

"Then we can plan for a June wedding. Wisconsin weather should be very nice then."

"Ooh, that's a good plan—the sooner, the better."

The two enjoy their dinner and listen to the Western music being played, Kenny Rogers's "The Gambler."

"How appropriate," Yolanda starts.

"What?"

"That song and just what we are trying to do. We are gambling with our futures, trying to find a way to save those little baby boys from being sacrificed for their prototensin, aren't we?"

"Yes, honey, we should really know about when to fold and when to run. Yet we cannot escape from the moral obligation that we must do now that we have enough circumstantial evidence."

"Bill, circumstantial evidence won't do. We need the smoking gun."

"Yes, and that is in the red room. Did you ever see one of those couriers enter the red room from your biochem lab?"

"Never. I see them enter and leave Westerman's office every now and then."

"So there has to be a way for the prototensin to reach the red room from Westerman's office."

"I've been to Westerman's office only sporadically just to pick up paperwork and such. Never had time to look around and see what's in it."

"I'll tell you what I'll do, Yolanda. I'll make an appointment to see Rodger Eastwood at his office, and together we might just be able to examine a foundation blueprint."

"We must come up with a good reason to do that."

"Leave that to me. You are in good hands now." He cups his hands, mimicking an Allstate Insurance commercial.

They enjoy their dessert as a group of other waiters and waitresses surround them, singing congratulations to the tune of the birthday song.

On their way out the door, Yolanda asks, "Bill, suppose we do get to see the blueprint from Eastwood, what do we do next?"

"I really don't know, Yolanda, but that is a job we need to do first!"

At this point Johnny Paycheck's song comes on the speakers: "Take This Job and Shove It!"

Bill turns his head toward the source of the music.

"Screw you!"

Laughing, they head toward their parked car.

CHAPTER 32

Eastwood's Office

EASTWOOD'S OFFICE IS AN IMPRESSIVE antebellum building in the center of Charleston. His suite is on the second floor, overlooking the heart of the city.

Rodger happily greets Bill and Yolanda.

"I expected to get this call from you sooner. I was just recently on the phone with Dave Westerman."

Bill and Yolanda look at each other anxiously.

"Oh?" Yolanda asks.

"Yes. It looks like you guys are going to be building an addition to the existing structure for something like a Ronald McDonald temporary housing for guests at the foundation."

Bill and Yolanda breathe a sigh of relief.

"Will it be attached to the old building, Rodger?"

"Well, it can very well be, depending on its size. You have room enough for a similar-sized building on the lot. Let me show you the blueprint of the current building."

"Will we need to shield that addition from whatever radiation is going on in the old building?"

Yolanda squeezes Bill's hand softly.

"Oh yes, definitely, that is city code. Let me take you to our blueprint room and show you what you have there, assuming that nothing had been added after it was first constructed."

They move into another section of the office. Rodger pulls out a rolled-up blueprint and unrolls it on a large table.

"We are worried about the radiation part."

"And rightfully so, Yolanda."

"Here is the radiation room as it was originally."

Rodger points to a section on the third floor.

The three of them look it over with keen interest.

Yolanda narrows in on a small area on one side of the room.

"What's this?"

"It's an electrically powered dumbwaiter."

"Where does it go?"

"Let's look at the other floor plan."

"Here, it goes behind a closet on the second floor and into this large office on the first floor."

"Westerman's office?"

"I don't know who has that office on that side of the building."

"How big is that dumbwaiter, Rodger?"

"Let us measure it." Rodger checks the measurement on the blueprint.

"It looks as if it is three feet by four feet."

"How much weight can something like that carry?"

"Maybe a good two hundred pounds, no more."

"I really have never seen a dumbwaiter, but it is fascinating."

"Rodger, did Westerman give you some kind of a time frame when construction should start?"

"He figured within the next couple of months or so, Yolanda."

"I wouldn't be surprised if the next project after that at the foundation would be to enlarge the facility itself. We see more and more patients each day."

"You are probably right. But we will need to tackle the projects one at a time. I'll give Westerman a call, probably in a couple of weeks or so, and meet with him here."

Bill and Yolanda look over the blueprint one more time and move away from the table.

"Rodger, thank you very much for seeing us today."

"You are welcome. Was I helpful?"

"Yes. I was just wondering where the planned addition was to be located. I thought it should be on the opposite side of the current structure, Rodger."

"I thought about that too, but that will take too much space from the area where the parking lot is located, Yolanda. And moving the parking lot to the other side will cost more and will make it too close to the next building, which will be against city code."

"Oh, I see. Thanks again, and do please give our love and regards to Adriane."

"Thanks for your visit, and have a great day."

Bill and Yolanda easily find their way out of the office and get back to their car.

CHAPTER 33

Roller's Apartment

BILL STUDIES A COPY OF the St. Bonaventure Hospital Medical Staff's Rules and Regulations. He has just come home from his office. The sound of a key working his front-door lock distracts him. Sensing trouble, he arms himself with a bottle of Coke, ready to clobber whoever it is. Yolanda enters and quickly settles on a comfortable sofa nearby, ignoring Bill.

"My key stuck. I needed to work it out."

"You look like you are out of breath, what's the matter?"

"After our meeting with Rodger yesterday, when he told us that Westerman had called him ahead of us, I felt like everybody at the foundation was about ready to hang me. I felt sneaky, but for good reason."

"Take it easy, honey. Nobody is after us...yet."

"Bill, eight—yes, eight—couriers were at the foundation this morning, which means that thirty-two babies were sacrificed to get this morning's supply of prototensin. We have to do something and soon."

"I've been looking into the hospital's rules and regs for something that might help us start. The only trouble is that the only name I recognize is Jules Pendergast's, and he is dead. I don't know who Adriane's obstetrician is."

Yolanda looks at Bill's stack of medical journals with his name clearly stamped on the covers.

"I never knew that you had a Spanish middle name."

"Brazilian. And that is my mother's maiden name. And come to think of it, is Ybarra your ex's last name?"

"And it is about time you know, lover boy. I annulled my marriage a year after Paul left me. Ybarra is my birth last name."

"I'd like to know your middle name."

"Are you ready for this?"

"Shoot."

"Yolanda Perpetua Milagros Ybarra y Virginia."

"Holy kashmoly!"

"No, Yolanda Perpetua Milagros Ybarra y Virginia."

"Our marriage license will have to have a second line to hold all that."

"They'll just have to make it fit. My mother prayed for a baby girl to the miraculous Virgin Mary of Perpetual Help, and she got me!"

"That makes sense."

"Did you find anything in that book you were reading?"

"No."

"Do you know a Dr. Gandt from the hospital?"

"I only know of him because he gave us a talk on hypertension once. He is a nephrologist, but he is not on our staff. Why?"

"I ran into a friend of mine who is a court reporter."

"And?"

"She told me that Dr. Gandt had given testimonies as expert witness on several malpractice and unethical suits around the county. He just may be the one to help us expose the foundation. He is very prolife and an excellent speaker."

"*Expose* is an awful dangerous word, sweetheart. We need to get into that damn room to get our smoking gun."

"Okay," Yolanda says with a bit of anger. "Tomorrow I will calmly walk into Westerman's office, demand the key to the room from him, and tell him that it is about time they stop killing babies and to take me to the damn red room where I can get all the evidence I need to put him and Davidson in prison forever!"

"Ooh, you do look lovely when you are mad! Do that again, please. It enhances your beautiful features."

"Please, please, Bill, I am serious!"

"Okay. I will get an appointment for us to see Gandt tomorrow, Wednesday afternoon, after my office. I'll have to find out where his office is."

"It might be in Mount Pleasant."

Yolanda notices a bucket of Kentucky Fried Chicken on Bill's kitchen table.

"Regular or crispy?"

"Extra crispy, and you are invited to a fancy home-cooked dinner with me."

"That will be a wholesome change from the marvelous restaurant dinners we have had lately—home-cooked."

Bill takes out paper plates and plastic silverware from a kitchen drawer, and the two enjoy their chicken dinner.

CHAPTER 34

Dr. Steven Gandt's Office
Mt. Pleasant, South Carolina

WELL-DRESSED AND DIGNIFIED, LOOKING LIKE a descendant from an old Southern plantation family, Steven Gandt receives them cordially at his office.

"Thank you, Dr. Gandt, for taking some time to see us today."

"Bill, just call me Steve, okay?"

"Okay, and by the way, your hypertension talk at the hospital was very well received, Steve."

"I try to be as clear as possible especially to the nurses and other nonphysicians. Where is your office, Bill?"

"In North Charleston."

"And I understand that you, Yolanda, work at the Davidson Cancer Research Foundation."

"Yes, Dr. Gandt."

"Steve, please."

"Yes, Steve."

"That place must be simply fabulous, what with all your success in treating terminal cancer patients. Do you preselect your patients?"

"In a way, Steve. We select only patients with undifferentiated cell carcinomas. They are the most responsive to the transforming factor gamma cytokine that we use."

"Transforming factor…?"

"Gamma."

"I am sorry, but being a nephrologist, I am not familiar with that cytokine, Yolanda."

"And that's the reason we are here."

"I don't understand."

Gandt starts looking at books in his bookcase for cytokine.

"You will not find it there, Steve."

"Then you will need to educate me, Bill."

"They are not using transforming factor gamma as they claim. They are using prototensin."

"I am not familiar with that one either."

"Prototensin is a cytokine that is, so far, the strongest known cancericidal in the world. We just learned that from Dr. Guthrie at UCSF."

"Wow, where do you guys get that prototensin? Do you synthesize that by irradiating horse nerve tissue or buy it from a laboratory not currently approved by the FDA?"

"No, Steve, we, meaning the foundation, are extracting that from the minced hypothalami of aborted first-pregnancy male human fetuses."

"What?" Steve looks aghast and horrified. "Good Lord, that can't be true!"

"Unfortunately, it is true. Steve, Yolanda and I saw the effect of prototensin on mice melanoma cultures at UCSF. Dr. Guthrie so nicely showed us. Not only that, but also for the cytokine to be effective, extracts from four different hypothalami are needed to cure the terminal cancer of a single mouse."

"If prototensin is as effective as you guys claim, then why do you even have failures at the foundation?"

"Because not all our patients get the prototensin treatment—only the important clients."

"What do the failures get?"

"Surgigel injections."

"Surgigel?"

"Surgigel is an inert, gelatinous solution that does not harm or do any good to patients. And they are each charged ten thousand dollars for the useless injections."

"Good Lord, may I ask you where you get this supply of hypo-thalami, Yolanda, from abortion clinics? Do women sell their unborn babies to the foundation? What is this world turning into?"

"Let me answer your questions, Steve, from all the information Yolanda and I have now."

"Okay, Bill. I am very angry."

"Physicians all over the country, I guess, abort male fetus carried by women in their first pregnancies at about the sixteenth or eigh-teenth week of gestation by giving them Zyatol disguised as special vitamin pills without the women being aware of what they really are."

"Zyatol?"

"Similar to RU-486."

"Good heavens!"

"Somehow, these doctors obtain the fetal hypothalami from the aborted fetuses and store them in a freezer until they can get four separate samples."

"Now then you are also implying that the pathologist perform-ing the autopsy on the fetus is in cahoots with them! That is simply preposterous!"

"I don't know, but obviously, they have to have the hypothalami for their scheme to work."

"Go on."

"As soon as they get the necessary number, four at the least, they send the hypothalami packed in dry ice via special couriers to the foundation."

"I have heard Westerman and Davidson talk about paying somebody sixty thousand dollars for a set of four," Yolanda adds.

"I think I've heard all that I need to hear. This has to be stopped!"

"And that is why we are here. We need your help, Steve."

"And I wish the world I could."

"Steve, we cannot simply go to the police and—"

"Oh no, they will probably put you in jail and keep you there until a psychiatrist can prove you sane."

"And that psychiatrist could be paid by the foundation."

"That might be a hell of a lot better than being eliminated by goons hired by the foundation."

"Okay then, what do we do next?"

"First, let me tell you my position. I chair the ethics committee of the county medical society. And I believe Davidson is not even a member of the society."

"So?"

"If we can prove that their failures are truly getting placebo injections and not prototensin as they claim, that in itself is one hundred percent malpractice. But then who knows about this besides you two?"

"Nobody but the three of us now."

"Yolanda, if you can secretly stash away a sample of the gelatinous material without prototensin and get it to a laboratory for examination and if the laboratory is not able to detect the presence of prototensin in the sample, then we have a definite case of malpractice."

"Which means taking the sample all the way to Dr. Guthrie in San Francisco."

"Whichever facility is equipped enough to analyze and recognize prototensin."

"Wow, what a task. Can you think of another way?"

"The only other person who comes to my mind is Harlan Hargrove."

"I don't believe I know him."

"His office is in Columbia. He is president of the medical society there, but he also belongs to the state licensing board. He might know how to figure out a way to start a process through the state board because his voice is strong enough at the state level."

"Okay. We will talk to Hargrove."

"Keep this information to yourselves. Tell Hargrove that you approached him because of his strong connection with the state licensing board and not because I sent you."

"I will give him a call right away."

"His phone should be listed in the directory. Thank you two for coming, and God bless you. You are true Christians."

"Thanks for your time. Goodbye."

CHAPTER 35

Harlan Hargrove's Office

IT IS ALMOST CLOSING TIME for offices in Downtown Columbia when Bill and Yolanda reach Hargrove's office. His office is the only posh suite in a building built for a multispecialty group of physicians. Its outside appearance is only matched by the decor inside, featuring paintings similar to what one might see only at the Louvre. Looking disheveled and tired from a full day's work, he apologizes as he welcomes Bill and Yolanda.

"I'm sorry to look like this, but I spent the whole night last night in the delivery room at the hospital. Will you two please sit down?"

Hargrove leads them to two comfortable couches in his office. They start a conversation on the way to their seats. On a wall, above a glass-covered medicine cabinet, Yolanda notices a framed etching on leather of a knight in armor, carrying a spear, on horseback. Behind the knight is a windmill.

"Thank you for seeing us, Dr. Hargrove. I am Bill Roller, and this is my friend, Yolanda Ybarra."

"Please just call me Harlan. When I got your call yesterday, Bill, I was a little confused at what you were trying to tell me. Yolanda, I can see that you are an art critic."

"I'm sorry, Harlan, but that framed etching looks a little odd to me. If this was set in Spain, then the windmill is out of place. Is that etched on leather?"

"I think that's supposed to be Don Quixote, but my wife got that when we were in Madrid two years ago. And yes, it is etched on leather."

"We do have a very serious problem facing us, Harlan, and we think that only a physician on the state licensing board may be able to help us."

"Some kind of...malpractice, Bill?"

"Worse, Yolanda and I consider this a case of infanticide...and on a grand scale!"

His face turning red, Hargrove explodes, "What, in heaven's name, are you talking about?"

"Harlan, I work as a medical technologist at the Davidson Cancer Research Foundation."

"Go on."

"We have been made to assume that our patients are being treated with transforming factor gamma, which is extracted by irradiating horse nerve tissue."

"Yolanda, I am not an oncologist, and I know nothing about transforming factor gamma."

"Harlan, transforming factor gamma does not exist."

"Now, you two have me confused. If this factor does not really exist, then what are you using at the foundation, Yolanda?"

"They use a cytokine known as prototensin," Bill interrupts.

"Proto...what?"

"Prototensin."

"Goodness gracious, you guys sound like Disney characters to me." Harlan scratches the back of his head.

"What, how...do you know all this, if it is true?"

"Okay, this is what Yolanda and I have pieced together."

"Do tell me before I lose my composure."

"The male fetuses of first pregnancies, at sixteenth or eighteenth week of gestation, concentrate this cytokine in their hypothalami."

"How does that happen?"

"Via an antigenetic fetal overexpression to a genetically inspired maternal hybridization that occurs only at initial gestation."

"Please, please don't repeat that. I am torn between throwing you both out of my office or allowing you to talk. You two could be dangerous."

"I see. It was a mistake for us to come to see you, Harlan. You don't have to throw us out. We will go quietly."

"No, please stay. There could be something in what you are saying. Let us start with this...this prototensin. How did you find out about this?"

"Yolanda gave me a tour of the foundation, for interest's sake, being a new family practitioner in North Charleston. When she mentioned transforming factor gamma, I was intrigued because that term was completely new to me."

"Go on."

"We made a search for it at the medical school library, but we were unable to find it. Still being interested in the current, most effective treatment for cancer, we continued searching, and we found this new cytokine prototensin."

"And this prototensin can be taken from the hypothalami of male fetuses."

"Yes, first-pregnancy male fetuses."

"That is completely amazing, but absolutely horrifying. But how do you know that it is from the hypothalamus and not kidney or liver or something else?"

"We went all the way to see Dr. Guthrie at UCSF. She is the only researcher in the United States doing research on prototensin."

"Harlan, couriers deliver the hypothalami to the center and hand them directly to Mr. Westerman."

"Who is Westerman?"

"Davidson's partner, who, we believe, pays for the prototensin we use at the foundation."

"Okay, let me say this. Your story could be all hogwash, but, Bill, you would not risk your reputation on a story like this."

"Heavens, no, Harlan."

"I think I might be able to help you. First, let us keep this...this story to ourselves."

"Okay."

"This is what I plan to do. Since we do not have foolproof evidence, I will bring it up with a select investigative committee of the state medical board.

"We might need to plant members or spies at your foundation, Yolanda. You will need to help them secretly obtain samples of that liquid that you inject the patients.

"As soon as we have collected enough samples, we might need to go to Dr. Guthrie at UCSF to analyze them, if she is the only one who can do it in the country. If we can prove that some samples contain prototensin while others do not contain prototensin, we will have a case against the foundation. A thorough investigation of the whole thing will then be necessary."

"Oh, Harlan, you don't know how much you have helped us!"

"Bill, Yolanda, I deeply share your concern about aborting otherwise-normal pregnancies. I am an obstetrician, and I practice my profession with the greatest morality and dedication. To me, there is nothing more rewarding than seeing a pregnant woman deliver her healthy baby safely and comfortably."

"Thank you, Harlan. Yolanda and I can go to sleep tonight knowing that something will and can be done to stop the sacrifice of poor, innocent babies."

Ending their meeting, Hargrove politely leads them out the office door.

As soon as Bill and Yolanda are out of sight, Hargrove picks up the phone. He dials a number.

"Arch Frankle?"

"Yes."

"Harlan here. I have distressing news for you. You need to act fast."

Chapter 36

Downtown Bar Charleston
Late Afternoon

FOWLER SCHMIDT SITS ON A barstool alone, holding his midsection tightly. In front of him is a bubbling glass of seltzer. A bartender approaches.

"Fowler, can I bring you something else? That seltzer isn't helping you any, or is it?"

"Oh, it is, it's just taking a little longer this time."

"I really hesitated to give you that last double vodka tonic."

"Hey, man, I enjoyed every drop of it."

Just then the phone rings, and the waiter answers.

"Hey, Fowler, this call is for you."

The waiter hands the phone to Fowler.

"I knew I'd find you there."

"Good afternoon, Dr. Frankle. What can I do for you, sir?"

"Don't you ever mention my name when talking to me on the phone again, you understand?"

"I'm sorry, sir. Yes, I'll definitely remember that."

"We have a job for you, and this time we need you to act fast and do your job any which way you want it done. We need you to take care of two clients."

"As you wish, sir. Double pay!"

"Yes, just do it ASAP."

CHAPTER 37

Interstate 26 South Carolina

ELATED, BILL AND YOLANDA DRIVE away as storm clouds darken the skies. Always enjoying a ride and scenery, they hope to beat the rain home.

"Oh boy, that was a relief."

"Yes, Yolanda. Getting that job out of our hands and sharing it with good, trustworthy medical people are, indeed, a huge relief. Hargrove looks like the idol of honesty."

"Now, don't tell me that this makes you hungry."

"Relieved as I am right now, I can eat a whole cow. I like his plan of getting the state board in on it. He is truly a gentleman ready to assist us in any way.

And oh, by the way, I didn't realize that you were an art critic! You stared at that picture of the knight quite intently."

"I thought I saw something peculiar about that windmill in the etching..." Yolanda lets out a horrifying scream. "Holy shit! Oh my god, my god, my god! Stop the car, Bill!"

Bill moves the car out of traffic and stops it.

Weeping loudly, Yolanda screams at Bill, "Your idol of honesty is nothing but a...a goddamn son of a bitch!"

"What are you talking about?"

"I remember what I saw inside that medicine cabinet below the knight's picture."

"What?"

"Zyatol! Zyatol! Dozens of them! Oh god, we just shared our secret with our most dreaded enemy. We are doomed! Doomed! Doomed!"

With clenched fists, Bill responds, "Why, that goddamned son of a bitch!"

"Isn't that what I just said? What, in heaven's name, are we going to do now? Before we are treated to the same fate as poor old Jules Pendergast?"

"Sweetheart, whatever it is, we need to do it fast."

Bill eases the car back into traffic on their way home.

"Bill."

"I'm still here."

"I'm scared to sleep in my apartment tonight."

"Why don't we stop by your place, pick up a few things, and we both stay in my apartment tonight? I'll sleep on my comfortable large sofa."

"What a gentleman, thank you."

"Hey, if anybody comes in, I will clobber him first before he gets to you in the bedroom, then."

"You know, that does make sense to me now."

"I keep on remembering what that big horse's ass said to me, 'There is nothing more rewarding than seeing a pregnant woman deliver her healthy baby safely and comfortably.' That damn, damn fake. I hope God heard him when he said that."

"I know He did."

CHAPTER 38

Roller's Apartment Nighttime, Same Day

As soon as Bill and Yolanda get to Bill's apartment, they barricade themselves in so tightly that a small army will have difficulty coming in.

"Yes, Yolanda, as Julius Caesar once said, 'I have crossed the Rubicon.' We have crossed our Rubicon, and there is no turning back now."

"Shall I go to work tomorrow?"

"Definitely. Just be on the lookout for anything unusual. I will be in my office and will also be watching out for anything unusual."

"Let me try to fix us something to eat before we go to bed—perhaps, something light. I am not very hungry."

"For a guy who enjoys eating, I am not starving either."

Yolanda finds salami and cheddar cheese in the refrigerator.

"Bill, how'd you like salami and cheese for dinner? Do you have crackers?"

"Since you cannot whip up chateaubriand in a jiffy, that'll do. I have Coke and local beer in the fridge too. Yes, crackers are in the cupboard."

"Honestly, Bill, what do we do now?"

"Believe it or not, I do have a plan."

"Thank God, would you mind sharing your daring plan with me?"

"Okay, we undoubtedly need the smoking gun."

"From the red room."

"Yes. If Hargrove has informed Davidson about us already, he might deactivate your entry code to the building. We need to get into the building before he does that."

"That makes sense although that will take some time to do. He will need to ask me to surrender my card, which will make it too obvious, or deactivate all the other cards except mine, which will take time."

"So we don't need to worry about that."

"No, I don't think so."

"Not for the time being. So now, we get into the building at night—tomorrow, which is Friday night. Remember, we have crossed the Rubicon."

"Oh god. We will need to start praying the rosary and now."

"Yes, we should've been doing that before we saw Hargrove."

"Bill, please continue."

"Okay, do you still have access to Westerman's office?"

"As far as I know, yes."

"The prototensin needs to be kept frozen, so we expect to see a freezer inside the red room. We will need to carry with us a small icebox, penlight, and camera."

"Camera?"

"Yes, to take pictures of whatever we can find in the logbook, such as doctors' names, locations, and whatnot."

"Do we try the dumbwaiter in Westerman's office to get to the red room?"

"I will first try to see if we can get in by using credit cards, a knife, or whatever we could find. We will use that only if nothing else works. I am afraid that even if the dumbwaiter looks big enough and can carry almost two hundred pounds, there is a small chance that you might get stuck."

"I never thought of that. Okay, granting that we are successful and still alive after our covert operation, what do we do with the evidence we will have obtained?"

"Elementary, my dear Watson. We freeze the hypothalami right here in my freezer, get all the pictures printed, and take them to Dr. Gandt."

"Okay, Mr. Holmes, are you sure Gandt is safe? We thought Hargrove was our man."

"I'm guessing that a nephrologist, specializing primarily in hypertension, will have nothing to do with obstetrics. Another option is to bring our smoking gun all the way to Dr. Guthrie."

"Oh lord, let us stick with the first one, win or lose."

"Okay, now we move my couch right there, against the door. I'll sleep there tonight. You take my bed. If anybody tries to enter the door, he will not only have to break the lock, but also move me too."

The two get ready to go to bed. Both are wary of the events that await them the next day.

Later that evening, Fowler Schmidt watches the entry to Bill's apartment building from his car. Having no way of entering the building, he sees one of the residents coming out and quickly enters before the door has the time to close.

Checking the mailboxes where Roller's apartment number 446 is listed, he makes his way up. Seeing no one about, he tries to turn the knob before using his knife to slip the lock.

A disheveled young man wearing hospital scrubs under his trench coat, coming down the hall to another apartment, sees him.

"Hey, if you are looking for Dr. Roller, he is not there. He is in Columbia with his girlfriend and probably staying there overnight."

"Thank you, sir. I'll just catch him at his office tomorrow morning." Schmidt leaves.

Having no idea how close the danger is, Bill and Yolanda sleep through the event taking place just outside their door.

CHAPTER 39

DCRF

IT IS A BRIGHT AND sunny Friday morning in Charleston. From a window in the animal laboratory Manny Timmerman watches very peaceful demonstrators outside the building. Carrying the usual placards, they walk around, sing, and give away candies and balloons. Some of them even help old and weak patients get in and out of the building.

He was able to get into the building with the suitcase containing the contraption without being noticed. Believing that it is still too early to set it up, he hides it under some rags behind the brooms and other equipment inside the storeroom.

On the biochemistry lab floor, Elaine keeps admiring the beautiful new ring that Yolanda is wearing as she pipettes out precipitates from test tubes.

"I... I've never seen so beautiful an engagement ring before. My mom has a dinner ring with an emerald surrounded by little diamonds. She knows that when the time comes, I will inherit that ring. Do you and Bill have wedding plans in the near future?"

"Not yet, Elaine. I don't think we are ready for that."

Just then they see Davidson in the hallway, coming right at them. Yolanda turns ashen briefly. "G-good morning, Dr. Davidson." Davidson notices Yolanda's concerned look.

"Good morning, Yolanda, Elaine. Yes, every peaceful demonstration we have had has been followed very shortly by severe and violent ones. You have reason to be concerned. But just be extra,

extra careful. Nobody has been hurt yet, but you never know. Suspect anybody and everybody looking suspicious."

Yolanda breathes a sigh of relief. "Thank you, sir. We will certainly watch out."

Work goes on peacefully inside the building with patients getting their injections as scheduled. The laboratory is alive with medical technologists and technicians going on with their work. On the first floor, Westerman receives several couriers coming from different parts of the country. They are likewise unhindered by the people demonstrating outside.

In the late afternoon Fowler Schmidt steps out from the elevator and heads directly to Yolanda and Elaine. He is dressed as an equipment technician or engineer.

He has with him his decorated straight walking stick. Lying to Yolanda, he speaks, "Ma'am, are you Ms. Ybarra?"

"Yes."

"Mr. Westerman downstairs has asked me to check your centrifuge."

"Elaine, is there anything wrong with our centrifuge?"

"I don't know. I don't think so." Elaine shakes her head.

Schmidt positions himself behind Yolanda, trying to stab her on her calf with his walking stick. Before he can get into a proper position, Yolanda moves away to take Schmidt to the centrifuge.

"Mr. Schmidt, here is our centrifuge. You are welcome to look it over."

Schmidt pretends to check the centrifuge, sometimes tapping it with his walking stick. He moves toward Yolanda again.

"How long have you had this machine?" He maneuvers into position again, occasionally grasping his midsection as if in pain.

"I know that it is over five years old. Are you all right, Mr. Schmidt?"

"Yes. My ulcer gives me trouble every once in a while." He walks a little closer to Yolanda to position his walking stick.

Just then they see Bill coming down the hallway toward them from the elevator. Yolanda walks away to meet Bill. Still grasping his midsection, Schmidt goes back to the centrifuge and pretends to look it over very carefully.

"Hello, Yolanda, Elaine."

"You certainly look like the happiest man in the world, Bill. You two must have set up a very special date already."

"Not yet, Elaine. Yolanda, are you about ready to go?"

"You bet."

Schmidt hurriedly follows them into the elevator. There he tries to stab Bill on his calf, but misses as the door opens and other passengers push Bill away to exit.

He tries to do the same to Yolanda, but all of a sudden he slumps forward, grasping his midsection, and writhes in severe pain, losing his walking stick in the process.

"Are you all right, Mr. Schmidt? You look very pale."

"Bill, this is Mr. Schmidt, technical engineer. He is here to check on our centrifuge. Mr. Schmidt, meet Dr. Roller."

"I have an ulcer, Dr. Roller."

"Mr. Schmidt, you are in such pain that the ulcer might have perforated."

"I hope not."

"Downstairs, we will call 911 for you so that they can take you to the hospital."

Schmidt is now in such pain that all he can do is agree with them. Bill picks up the stick and saves the unusual piece to give it back to Schmidt later.

In a few minutes an ambulance arrives in front of the center. Paramedics come in pushing a gurney and, after a preliminary check of blood pressure, etc., take Schmidt out of the building on a gurney with them.

Both Davidson and Westerman thank Bill and Yolanda for their assistance. None of them know that Schmidt was hired by Archibald Frankle to kill both Bill and Yolanda.

Upstairs, the animal caretakers have also left the building except Manny Timmerman. He is setting up the contraption that Jason Janz gave him. He selects a place inside the equipment closet behind pails and tanks on the floor as close to the wall as possible.

It is as far away from his beloved animal cages as can be.

It is close to their dissecting and examination table where, he figures, it will cause the most destruction with the least possible injury to the animals he so loves.

He sets the timer to go off at 1:00 AM. He covers it up with rags and rolls of paper towels. He has no idea of the magnitude of the contraption he is about to unleash.

CHAPTER 40

Nighttime

FROM THE CAR THAT BILL and Yolanda parked on the far side of the foundation's lot, they can clearly see the front entrance to the darkened building.

"Yolanda, perhaps, we should park where we can see the back entrance."

"Not yet. I'd like to see if, perhaps, somebody is still in the building, who hasn't left through the front entrance."

"It's past eleven, Yolanda. Who could possibly still be working in there?"

"Okay, then let's go to the other side of the building."

"You are sure you can come in and disarm the system at this time, huh?"

"Oh, I think so."

"You better know so."

They wait another fifteen minutes, leave their car, taking with them their small icebox, and get into the building by the back, using Yolanda's card. She also disarms the alarm system. It works like clockwork.

Using a penlight and whatever light filters in from the outside, they walk up the steps to the door of the red room.

Bill uses his credit card to no avail, a penknife, and other sharp items he can find, but is still unable to open the door.

"I'd make a rotten thief."

They walk back down to Westerman's office.

Yolanda confidently turns the doorknob. It is locked.

"Darn it. He never locks his door."

"Perhaps, he was expecting something today. Let me try to open it with my card."

After several swipes, the lock does give, and the knob turns. They enter the room very cautiously and quietly, using their penlight to go directly to the dumbwaiter—so far, so good.

The door to the dumbwaiter opens easily.

Yolanda takes her shoes off and very carefully eases herself into the dumbwaiter with Bill giving her a gentle push time and again.

"Yes, and keep quiet. Now, push that green button, and wait outside the red room. I'll open the door as soon as I get up there."

"Okay."

Bill waits outside the red room. After ten minutes, which felt like forever, he goes back down to Westerman's office. Yolanda is stuck.

"What the hell took you so long to get back here? I'm stuck."

"Sorry, I know we are both scared and frustrated, let me see what I can do."

Bill searches the side of the dumbwaiter and finds two thick, white cords, one on each side of the dumbwaiter. He pulls on the one located to the right; nothing happens. He pulls on the one on the left, and the dumbwaiter moves up, but only a couple of inches.

"Honey, can you reach this cord?"

"You've got to be kidding, sweetheart, that one is behind me."

Bill helps Yolanda ease herself completely out of the dumb-waiter. She takes a deep breath and, with Bill's help, eases herself back in, this time facing the other way. Once inside, she takes hold of the cord.

"Bill, push that green button as I pull this cord, okay?"

Sure enough, the dumbwaiter slowly rises and keeps on rising as long as the two of them are working together simultaneously. The green light turns off as soon as the dumbwaiter reaches the third floor. As soon as the light is off, Bill hurries up the steps to the red room and waits for the door to open.

With great difficulty, Yolanda extricates herself out of the dumb-waiter and, using her penlight, searches for the front door. She can also hear soft taps as Bill gives her a sign that he is outside.

She quickly opens the door and lets Bill inside. They are unaware that the door is specially alarmed to bedroom receivers in both Westerman's and Davidson's homes.

Both men wake up from their sleep, get dressed, and quickly arm themselves with 9mm Magnums. They leave for the foundation ASAP from their respective homes.

Using their penlights, the two search every corner of the red room. As they expected, they find no radiation equipment anywhere. They do find a large freezer with test tubes and vials filled with frozen hypothalami in groups of four, properly labeled with physicians' names and dates on them. A computer sits on top of a desk.

Bill carefully picks up a few of the vials and places them in their cooler. Yolanda finds a large logbook with physicians' names and addresses. She carefully takes pictures of every page with her small camera. She sees Hargrove's and Pendergast's names. It shows amounts of money paid to them in cash by the foundation and the dates. She makes sure that they are all photographed, taking several shots of each of the entries.

"Do we have everything we need from here?"

"I don't know, Bill. Do you have enough hypothalami samples in the cooler?"

"Yes."

"And I have enough pictures. Let's get out of here."

They quietly approach the door. Yolanda hears faint footsteps from outside coming closer and closer.

"Shh, Bill, somebody's out there."

Bill pulls Yolanda behind him and firmly positions himself close to the door and waits for the door to open. He sees someone stealthily nearing the door that is partially ajar, with a gun in his hand.

With the full force of his body weight he slams the door shut, crushing the arm. The gun drops to the floor. Davidson screams with pain outside the door. Yolanda searches for the gun, but cannot find it in the dark.

With his gun drawn, Westerman pushes a screaming Davidson into the room and enters behind him.

Bill slams a fistful of gelatin-filled glass vials, which he was able to quickly pick up from a nearby rack of tubes, into Westerman's face.

Temporarily blinded, Westerman fires his gun randomly.

Bill and Yolanda, cooler and camera in their possession, run toward the stairwell as Westerman recovers from his blindness. He fires several shots in the direction of the stairwell.

Bill and Yolanda turn away from the stairwell and head toward the biochemistry laboratory, with Westerman in hot pursuit, leaving Davidson groaning in the radiation room.

In the dark, Westerman fires at them while he searches for the light switch. Roller and Ybarra hide behind the laboratory furnishings to avoid being hit.

Westerman finds the light switch. The brightness exposes the corner of the laboratory where Bill and Yolanda are cowering.

Fuming with rage, Westerman approaches them, pointing his gun at Bill.

"So it is you and you, Yolanda!"

Behind him, Davidson slowly approaches, holding his crushed forearm. Inflamed with anger, he recognizes the two.

"I never did think I could trust you, Yolanda. What do you mean by this?"

"We now know exactly what you two are doing here, Dr. Davidson."

"And what do you know, Dr. Roller?"

"That you are using prototensin instead of the transforming factor gamma that you claim."

Davidson and Westerman look at each other.

Davidson starts, "I thought these punks were just thieves trying to steal medicines from us, Dave!"

"We will have to deal with you two in a way worse than you can possibly think. Shall we take them downstairs, Randy? Here, hold the gun on them, and I will tie them up."

He binds their hands and marches them down to the animal laboratory. They force them into one of the animal-operating sections, away from the animal cages.

Westerman shoves Bill to a corner and ties Yolanda down on a small operating table, her bound legs hanging off the end of it.

Yolanda yells, "How long do you think you can get away with murdering unborn babies to harvest your prototensin?"

"Simple," Davidson answers. "As long as we can get rid of people like you!"

"How did you ever find out about this prototensin?"

"Now that I know you'll never be able to spread the news, Dr. Roller, I discovered that while doing my PhD work in Germany using guinea pigs."

Davidson turns to Westerman. "Will you please prepare the gelatin solution that I have saved for using in an emergency situation like this?"

"Certainly, Randy."

Westerman brings down a gelatinous solution from the biochemistry laboratory. He draws a colorless fluid from a vial, using a syringe, and mixes it with the material.

"Dr. Roller, you may not recognize these solutions, but I just had Dave mix cyanide with Surgigel. The Surgigel binds the cyanide and releases it after your tissues have absorbed the Surgigel, which takes about, oh, four or five hours. We don't intend to immediately kill you two, you know."

"Why, you goddamn sons of bitches!"

"You will walk out of here looking unharmed. Get into your car, and in that amount of time, call police or whoever you want to inform before you two feel awfully uncomfortable, start blabbering fairy tales, and pass out. Nobody will be able to resuscitate you."

"Let me go, you demons!" Yolanda tries to get herself untied.

"Oh yes, Yolanda, as you see, the needle needs to be big enough and long enough because the solution is injected intraperitoneally right under your breastbone. We need not sterilize anything because you will be dead before any kind of infection can set in. It is also done without anesthesia."

Davidson turns to Westerman. "Dave, you do the injecting. I cannot bear to hear a woman scream."

Helplessly bound, Bill can do nothing but yell, "You goddamn sons of bitches!"

Westerman pulls Yolanda's dress up and exposes her belly up to right below her breasts. Helpless and bound, Yolanda screams and gazes at the tip of the needle on its way closer and closer to her abdomen.

Suddenly, a powerful explosion coming from the door to his left throws Westerman clear to the opposite side of the room, knocking down lamps, metallic poles, and cabinetry, killing him instantly on his way. It also throws the table with Yolanda on it, Bill, and Davidson to the area where the animal cages are located. Glass and surgical instruments are airborne; furniture and sections of oxygen tanks, combined with a raging fire, consume the room.

The blast creates a large hole on the side of the building. Fueled by ruptured oxygen tanks and gas lines that lead into the building, the fire begins to rapidly engulf the entire floor.

The table with Yolanda still tied to it is forced toward the animal cages. The impact frees her from the table, but breaks her ankle in the process.

"Bill, Bill, where are you? What happened?"

There is no answer. She sees fire burning at the end of the room where she was before.

"Bill, Bill, where are you?"

Bill regains consciousness.

"Yolanda, what happened?"

"I don't know, but can you get closer to me? Perhaps, we can get ourselves loose."

Inch by every painful inch, avoiding the crawling rats, mice, and fire, they work their way to get themselves freed from their bindings.

Bill notices the huge deformity on her left ankle.

"Honey, your ankle is broken, I will be as gentle as I can."

"It is also very painful, please."

He helps her get up onto her right leg.

Then they see Davidson, his face bloodied by a gash on his neck, lying unconscious with rats and mice crawling over him. Roller quickly checks him.

"He is still alive. Let's get him out of here."

"Where's Westerman?" Yolanda asks.

"I don't know."

They search for Westerman as spilled chemicals catch fire and emit a foul-smelling smoke.

"Yolanda, did you get that injection?"

She raises her dress. "No. I see no needle marks."

"Thank God."

They hear sirens coming from outside the building. Soon they feel the blast of cold water coming from firefighters controlling the fire. With the fresh water clearing the smoke and fire, they find Westerman's lifeless body under a metallic rack.

Firefighters are soon on the animal floor armed with picks, axes, and a large water hose. Finding people inside the building, they call out for stretchers to be brought in. They put Yolanda, Bill, and the unconscious Davidson on stretchers and carry them out of the building as rapidly as possible.

They also find Westerman. They cover his body with a sheet and carry it out of the building on a stretcher. The fire has nearly engulfed the entire building by the time the rescuers make their way out with the wounded Bill, Yolanda, and Davidson.

Several other firefighters assist in controlling the fire in an attempt to save the building.

The following morning police and firefighters cordon off the still-smoking gutted remains of principally the top of the building. The first floor miraculously escapes being heavily burned.

A woman and a teenage boy are staring at the crumbled site. He is in a wheelchair, looking pale, emaciated, and disappointed. She looks down at her son dejectedly.

"Honey, I just called Dad. We are flying home tomorrow."

"Mom, can I get my cancer shots anywhere around here?"

"I'm afraid not. It's just too bad, son, you have only one more week left in your treatment. I don't even know how your dad and I can get back the hundred thousand dollars we deposited for your treatments."

"Am I gonna die now, then?"

"Never, honey. Your dad and I will take you any place on earth to get you back to health again."

CHAPTER 41

Yolanda's Apartment

IT IS LATE AFTERNOON TWO days after the foundation building burned down. Yolanda entertains Bill, Jerry, and the pregnant Juanita in her apartment. Juanita has been taking care of her sister for a couple of days already. Her guests write their names on Yolanda's white left leg cast while she is seated on the couch. Her crutches lie within her reach.

"Bill, why did it take them much longer to treat you at the hospital? They were ready to push me out of there when you got your permission to leave. You said you only had scratches and minor burns."

"But I had a concussion. The head and neck X-rays took much longer to complete, you know. Are you still in a lot of pain?"

"No. Thank God."

"Bill, what's going to happen to Yolanda's job there?"

"The hospital is always looking for medical technologists, Juanita. I don't think that will be a problem. Besides, next June, she will have another job waiting for her."

"Bill, you keep quiet!"

"Oh, I'm sorry, Yolanda. I'm just so excited to tell your sister and brother-in-law that you are not wearing that ring for no good reason. Now you have to tell them yourself, honey."

"Okay, now that the secret is out, Bill and I are planning a wedding in Wisconsin next June, hopefully at Holy Hill."

"Whoopee! I'll be a maid of honor one more time! Besides, I'll have had the baby by then."

"Sis, are you being presumptuous?"

"Who else is crazy enough to be your maid of honor? Is that okay, Jerry?"

"Certainly."

"Then let me propose a toast for the three of you, and may God bless you!"

They look around for glasses and soft drinks in the kitchen.

"Bill, did the police tell you what caused that explosion there?"

"Jerry, they told me that the primary site was in a closet on the second floor of the building. It ripped that side of the building open and started a fire from ruptured gas lines and oxygen tanks. We were so lucky to have survived that."

"You two were at the building at night?"

"Yes, Jerry, it was a very busy Friday, and I was helping Yolanda finish things up in the biochemistry laboratory because they were expecting more than the usual number of patients for treatment the following Monday."

"Bill, I remember Davidson telling me and Elaine that a very peaceful demonstration means that something drastic is going to happen soon. He was right. There was an unusually peaceful demonstration that Friday morning. Is Dr. Davidson still in the ICU?"

"No, Yolanda. Davidson died on the way to the hospital."

"Oh, Bill, I just remembered what I meant to ask you. Do you still have Mr. Schmidt's cane? I want to show it to Jerry and Juanita because it looked so pretty and richly decorated."

"No. I was playing with it in my apartment, and I happened to push on a little daisy painted on it with a black center. A tiny needle came out of its tip, which retracted back when I released the pressure. I was concerned, so I took it to the police department for them to look at.

Earlier this afternoon a detective from the police department called me. He kept me on the phone for quite a while, asking me whose it was and where he is right now, among other questions. He was also making extra sure that I did not prick my skin with it or come close to it and not to tell Mr. Schmidt that they have it."

"Do you know where he is, Bill?"

"I think he is still at the hospital, but let me find out. If I remember correctly, I think I promised to give him back his cane."

CHAPTER 42

St. Bonaventure Hospital

BILL AND YOLANDA VISIT A recovering Mr. Fowler Schmidt. Bill is surprised to see that Schmidt is still on intravenous fluids and oxygen.

"How do you feel, Mr. Schmidt? Are you in much pain?"

"Thank you, Dr. Roller, for coming to see me. Did you bring my cane with you?"

"No, but I will save it until you are out of the hospital."

"Thank you. You know, I did have an ulcer like you said, but a really bad one."

"They...they took me to surgery that night that the ambulance brought me in."

He notices Yolanda wearing a cast and on crutches.

"I'm sorry, ma'am, but I didn't notice your cast right away, how did you get hurt?"

"It's a rather long story."

"You did say that you had a bad ulcer?"

"Yes, Dr. Roller. My surgeon told me that when he took me to surgery, he was really expecting to find a perforated ulcer that he could simply repair and that everything would be okay."

"Yes?"

"Well, they found a perforating cancer in my stomach. They closed it all right, but the cancer has already spread all over my belly, including my liver and spleen. They were not able to do anything surgically. It is a very aggressive type of stomach cancer."

"Good God!"

"My only hope now is to get treated at the Davidson Foundation. I know they can get me cured. I've saved enough money to pay for their treatment. Fortunately, I will not need to go too far to get my treatment. That seems to be my last hope now."

Bill and Yolanda look at each other.

"Mr. Schmidt...Fowler."

"Yes, Ms. Ybarra?"

"There was a big explosion at the center Friday night. It destroyed the building almost completely. Both Dr. Davidson and Mr. Westerman were killed."

Schmidt starts sobbing softly.

"Dr. Roller, where...where do you think I can get treated for my cancer?"

"Oh, I'm sure your surgeon will mention several options for you as soon as you have recovered from the surgery completely."

"Thank you, and thank you for coming by to see me."

Bill and Yolanda leave Schmidt's room. They pass by two uniformed police officers guarding his hospital room just outside the door.

Epilogue

Old Site, DCRF

One month after the destruction of the Davidson Cancer Research Foundation, Bill, Yolanda, Jerry, and Juanita, who is pushing a baby buggy with their precious baby boy, are watching engineers and other workers use large machinery to remove debris from the foundation site.

"I really don't know if I am pleased or not, but I had a good-paying job at that foundation. Now I am starting from ground zero as medical technologist at the hospital."

"Look, sis, you could have been killed there."

"Yes, Juanita. There wouldn't have been any chance for you to become maid of honor again."

"Oh, that's sad. Bill, what's going to happen now?"

"Well, Jerry, you remember that after we had all the pictures that Yolanda took in the red room printed, we met with Dr. Janz at his office. The book had the list of quite a number of physicians, how much they were paid in cash over the years, and the number of vials of prototensin, which means that the IRS will be going after those physicians. We also gave him the jar of Zyatol capsules that Juanita took before she had the miscarriage. Sadly, however, there was no list of the women's names whom they had purposely aborted to get the unborn male fetuses."

"Jerry, we also gave him all the frozen hypothalami that we recovered from the red room."

"Yes, Yolanda. There will be a thorough investigation about what took place at the foundation involving probably hundreds of physicians all over the country. The FBI has also been notified because there was a safe in Westerman's office, which the police were able to open.

Almost a million dollars in cash was found. They are looking into hidden funds for both Davidson and Westerman, both in and out of the country."

"Lorena may finally have some peace of mind as to what really happened to Dr. Pendergast."

"Oh yes, Yolanda, now that you mentioned Lorena, Fowler Schmidt also confessed. He was not able to take the guilt of murder with him to his grave. He is still alive, but now the stomach cancer has spread throughout his body. He told the police that a Dr. Frankle paid him to kill Dr. Pendergast. He would have been paid double had he been able to kill both you and me. We do feel good about stopping this killing field and can happily move on with our lives together. I love you."

ABOUT THE AUTHORS

URIEL R. LIMJOCO IS A general surgeon who retired from twenty years of private practice and twenty years of active surgical service to the United States Navy as well. In addition to his medical degree, he holds a master of science degree in physiology. He is a retired captain in the United States Navy and assistant clinical professor of trauma and general surgery from Loma Linda University. He is also a 100 percent disabled United States Navy veteran. He has published several articles of surgical nature in the *Annals of Thoracic Surgery, Canadian Journal of Surgery,* and *Wisconsin Medical Journal.* He is a retired member of several organizations including, but not limited to, the American

College of Surgeons, San Diego Society of General Surgeons, Los Angeles Surgical Society, and Milwaukee Academy of Surgery.

Carolyn Jo Limjoco met her husband, Uriel R. Limjoco, while she was in college at the University of Wisconsin in Madison. Her young married life was principally involved in raising their six children and leading them to become God-loving, educated, and industrious members of the community. Always principled in helping and educating less fortunate children, she spent many years as member of a school board in Wisconsin, ten of them as president. All the time she donated her salary for scholarship money to deserving students. She and her husband spent many years as a safe house for battered children in Wisconsin. She is well-read and had coauthored *The Story of the Hanford Horse* with Hank Meals for the Carnegie Museum in Hanford, California, when she was curator.

CPSIA information can be obtained
at www.ICGtesting.com
Printed in the USA
BVHW072013230321
603272BV00007B/840